Through the Fire

Books by Jordan Nasser

Home is a Fire

The Fire Went Wild

This Fire Inside

Home is a Fire Books 1-3

Through the Fire

Through the Fire

JORDAN NASSER

THROUGH THE FIRE

To all the people who cherished a kiss.

1

NO MORE DRAMA

Love can kiss my ass.

There he stood, smiling as if he didn't have a care in the world. But I knew he had to be at least as nervous as I was shocked. I hadn't expected him to show up like this, but here we were. Luke had decided to come to my parents' wedding after all, but I was pretty sure he hadn't thought past that point. One of us needed to do something quickly, and it seemed it was up to me.

"Hi," I said, looking him directly in the eyes. "My name is Derek."

"Hi. I'm Luke."

It was stupid, but it was ours. It was what we did when

it all went wrong and we had to find our way back. We started at the beginning.

"Listen, I don't…" I tried to say, but before I could utter another word, he lunged through the door frame and backed me up against the very same wardrobe door where we had found Fletch and Amber rolling around on the floor at her engagement party to Todd Carmichael just a few short weeks ago. Fletch's wife, Brandee, had seen the whole thing transpire and Fletch had gone back to New York City with his tail between his legs and his newly acknowledged son Jett following behind. To say I was happy he was out of our lives was an understatement. But the wreckage Fletch left behind was more than Luke and I could handle. Luke had said he needed space. And now it seemed he had finally come around. But was I expected to take him back, with no questions?

His hands grabbed mine as he interlocked our fingers and nudged me back against the heavy door. His breathing became intense and his heart pounded against my own as his lips grazed my neck.

"I don't…" I tried again unsuccessfully as I gasped for air before he covered my mouth with his. The kiss was both aggressive and loving at the same time. I could feel his passion, and I knew right then that he had longed for me as much as I had for him.

"Luke, I don't…"

"Stop *don'ting*." He had paused kissing me just long enough to speak two words before diving back in.

I held him tightly, moved my head to the side to avoid his attention and said, "That's not even close to being grammatically correct, babe."

"Mood killer." He didn't stop.

"I *love* this," I whispered. "I *missed* this, but I *don't* have the time." I placed both my hands against his broad chest. Wow. I had *really* missed that. "Dad is upstairs waiting for a bourbon so he can get over his fears of remarrying Mom, and she and Uncle Barry are holed up in the library waiting for the all clear sign. We have an entire patio full of guests waiting for a ceremony to begin. It's a wedding, remember? I've got *ish* to do."

Finally, he stopped kissing me.

"*Ish*?" He looked at me funny and cocked his head.

"What's wrong with *ish*?"

"Nothing, if you're, like, twenty-five."

"*Like?*" I teased.

"I'm a high school football coach, remember? I'm around kids all day."

"Yeah, well I've been living with Barry and his twenty-something boyfriend for the last few weeks. And Tucker's definitely taught me lots of *ish*. But maybe we could go over all of that after this little family wedding I'm trying to pull off? Deal?"

He smiled and laughed softly. The pressure was off. Or was it?

"It's a date. Let me get that bourbon for your dad. Neat or on the rocks?" He quickly walked behind the bar and grabbed a highball glass from the shelf and placed it on the bar mat.

"Neat," I answered with a cautious smile.

He poured a healthy dose and slid it across the seasoned dark wood surface to my waiting hands. Our fingers just barely grazed and I wanted to linger, but I knew I was about to get lost again and I didn't have the time. Not yet, at least.

"Listen," I said. "I want to do this. I want to talk. But don't expect me to go easy on you. Not after everything we've been through."

"I don't expect that at all," he said. "I'm coming into this with a clear head. I want to be open and honest. Being without you has been awful. I messed up and I want to fix this. If you'll let me."

I wanted to. I really did. But I had other pressing matters, like my parents, a drag queen, and half the town waiting in the other room. I had to refocus.

"Wedding, remember? Catch me after?" I asked, flirting

as if my life depended on it.

"You bet. I'm a friend of the family, so I intend to stick around."

"Well, all right then," I said, smiling. I turned to walk towards the upstairs office to grab my dad. I didn't dare turn back as I didn't want him to see the look of awe on my face.

Were we really doing this?

I was halfway across the black and white checkered dance floor when he cried out, "Hey!"

I stopped but didn't turn. "Yeah?"

"I love you."

"Good to know." And I kept on walking.

···

The wedding needed to go off without a hitch. Well, that wasn't quite the truth. Mom and Dad were about to *get* hitched after being apart for so many years. They had found each other again and I couldn't help but see the parallels in my own life.

But I had gotten ahead of myself, like always. Luke and I hadn't resolved anything yet.

I should probably stop mentally dialing U-Haul for my moving truck.

With the real mission in mind, I ran up the stairs two by two to deliver the bourbon to Dad.

"You ready, killer?"

"What's gotten into you?" he asked.

"Come on down, Johnny Ray. You're the next contestant on *The Bride is Right*!"

He downed his drink in one quick gulp and placed the empty glass on my desk.

"I'm never going to overcome Barry's influence in your life, am I?" he said with a smirk.

"Nope. Now let's go, cowboy. The dames are a waitin'."

He rolled his eyes and walked past me down the stairs to take his place at the makeshift altar in the garden. All of our friends were in attendance, and I could see them from where I stood at the doorframe. Shawn was ready to officiate, and Bammy, Michael, Tommy, Meredith, Kit and Tucker were already in their places. Even Peaches and the girls from Chesty Cheese were there.

Luke appeared behind me and I could feel the heat from his body before he had even said a word. I reached down instinctively with my right hand and softly tugged at his fingers as I pulled him up the aisle and we took our seats in the very first pew. I glanced behind me and Bammy signaled a wide-eyed thumbs up. Kit was so happy that one would have thought *she* was getting married, but her smile could always fill a room on even the greyest of days. She only had eyes for Shawn, and he was about to begin the ceremony. He looked at me and nodded that he was ready, then glanced over at Crosby and motioned for him to begin the music.

We all turned our heads and you could hear the audience gasp with delight as Uncle Barry's drag persona Beret stepped out in full regalia and began her march down the aisle. The speakers were playing an instrumental version of "Love Hangover" by Diana Ross, and if that didn't give us a clue that this was going to be the most non-traditional wedding ever, nothing would. Beret didn't come to play; she came to put on the show of all shows. Her shimmering grey satin gown was all pageantry and sparkles and she looked absolutely stunning. She walked down that aisle as if she had stepped onto the most important runway of her life, or at least the most extravagant drag ball in Harlem. Paris was indeed burning, children, and we were all in attendance. All eyes were on her and she knew it. She took her place in the front to Shawn's right and subtly winked at Tucker before regaining her composure. Beret was concentrating so hard on playing the part of the perfect maid of honor that she didn't even notice Luke sitting in the family pew right next to me. Well, at least she pretended not to notice. I was sure I would hear her opinion soon enough, though.

Crosby faded out Donna Summer and switched over to Mom's musical choice, "At Last," by Etta James as Shawn indicated for us all to rise. The audience stood and we turned around to watch Mom's dramatic entrance. When we were arranging all of this, I had assumed that she wanted me to walk her down the aisle, but she had other plans.

"I know it would make you happy, sweetie, but I've been doing things to please other people all my life," she told me. "It's about time I do something *by* myself, *for* myself."

I couldn't argue with that.

She floated down that aisle with grace and purpose and I had never been prouder of her. Had Barry given her pointers? I couldn't remember a time when I had seen her looking so lovely and content. Whatever she was doing, she was doing it right, and as she took her place next to my dad, I could see the tears start to form in his eyes.

"Please be seated," Shawn started, and we all took our places back in the pews. He took a deep breath, smiled at Mom and Dad, and then began. "Dearly beloved, we are gathered here today to get through this thing called life."

...

"Baby! *You. Killed. It!*" Kit grabbed Shawn and wrapped her arms around him as she reached up and kissed him on the cheek. "The best preacher man I know! I'm so proud of you!"

"Was it alright?" he asked us. You could see that he had been nervous at the beginning, but once he found his rhythm he coasted through the ceremony on a natural high full of adrenaline and love. "I really hope everyone enjoyed it. Y'all aren't just saying that, right?"

"You did great! We loved the Prince reference," said Bammy. "Maybe we'll need your services soon, now that this one is on the way." She rubbed her belly and smiled at Michael. He beamed right alongside her.

"Have you made any plans, yet?" I asked. "Because I just happen to know a great location…"

"We've talked it over with my parents, as well as Red and Rosa," Michael explained, "and Red wants to host the reception up at the Walcott mansion."

"Fancy!" said Kit.

"I'm into that," added Meredith. "Have you set a date?"

"Well, I don't want to be a pregnant bride," said Bammy. "That's just too much for me. Visions of shotguns are not my thing. I know my mother won't be too pleased, but it's definitely going to be after the birth. I couldn't decide which was worse. Having a kid and then getting married? Or trying to stuff this belly into a white wedding gown and having to pretend I look pretty?"

"I'd never have to pretend that, sweetheart," said Michael as he placed a romantic kiss on her lips.

"Get a room," said Tommy with a smirk. Meredith rolled her eyes at her boyfriend, but Luke tightened his grip on my hand. Was he thinking of tonight? Because at the moment, we didn't even officially live together anymore.

"Speaking of rooms…"

Damn it, Bammy. Couldn't you just let this one coast?

"What's going on here?" she asked, as her finger danced back and forth between me and Luke. "Don't get me wrong. We like it."

"We *love* it," Kit interjected.

"Yes, that!" she agreed. "But what happened? When, what, why, where and *how*?" she asked.

I could feel everyone's eyes on us as they all grew quiet, waiting for an answer.

"Let's save that for later," Luke said, as his eyes narrowed, and his charm came to the rescue once again. "Right now, let's just pretend it was all a dream."

"Like Bobby Ewing!" I said, gleefully.

"No one's going to get that reference, babe."

I smiled, defeated. He was right. This wasn't the time or the place, and we certainly weren't in *Dallas*. I always masked my nervousness with humor. But what had happened between us was most definitely not a dream. It was a nightmare. Maybe he had the right idea, though.

Could we really just let it all go?

***

"This was from Irma's Bridal, if you can believe that. Irma doesn't have a lot of great things, but every now and then you can find a real gem." Beret was recounting the story behind every piece she was wearing. "I picked up the jewelry at an estate sale. Tucker bought the clutch for me in Atlanta. And the shoes, well, I had to order those online. Tucker helped me with that, too. There aren't many women in Parkville who wear a size thirteen and a half, after all!"

"May I offer anyone a refill?" Sam approached us with a bottle of champagne to top us all off.

"Thanks for taking care of things," I said as he turned to head back to the bar. I saw Crosby passing hors d'oeuvres out of the corner of my eye.

"No problem, Boss. Enjoy! We got this."

Luke was still at my side. He hadn't really let go of my hand since before the service began. I didn't know what to think, yet, so I made myself think of something else. I had found my place here at the Duke. I'd instituted a lot of changes since taking over Lloyd's Catering and turning this place into my dream catering and event service. Getting away from the drama at the high school was exactly what I had needed to reestablish myself in Parkville. But getting off track with Luke had not been part of my plans.

"Well, I think you look fabulous," Kit told Beret, snapping me out of my reverie. "And I love that bag. *Have. To. Have!*"

"Tucker, where did we get this, again?"

Barry's life had changed enormously since his big coming out at the Love All event, back when Luke and I were challenging the conservative wave in Parkville. Though Tucker hadn't officially moved in, they were now secure enough in their relationship to be seen in public. Mom and Dad had welcomed Tucker into the family, so to speak, and all of my friends thought he was great. I had never seen Barry so happy, at least not since before my Aunt Janey had passed. He was a completely new man now. Well, the kind of man who could pull of a beaded gown and four-inch heels.

"Snap out of it, Nephew. You still with us?"

My eyes locked with my uncle's and I came back to reality.

"Sure thing," I said. Luke's grip on my hand remained firm. It felt like if he were to let go, he'd lose me forever.

"Let's go grab your parents, shall we?" said Beret. "It's picture time and this queen is ready for her close-up. Tucker, do be a doll and go grab my makeup kit? I need a little powder to dull this shine."

"That doesn't sound like you," said Tucker, laughing.

"Well, we all do what we need to do for the cameras, darling. But you know nothing will ever diminish my sparkle."

...

Aisha, the door girl from Parkville's favorite music venue the Bongo Room, was also an amateur photographer. Shawn had recommended her as we needed someone at the last minute. You may recall that we planned this whole thing in less than two weeks. Well, it turned out that not only did she have a great eye for detail, but she missed her calling in life as a fantastic cat herder. She took charge immediately.

"We're gonna start with Audrey by herself, then add

Johnny and the rest, one by one. Audrey, I want you to be the center of attention today, okay?"

"Well, I'm not really used to that," Mom demurred. "I'll do my best."

"You look beautiful," said Dad, from the sidelines.

He was right. She did look stunning. Aisha placed Mom by herself out in the garden and began snapping away. She added Dad alongside her, and then took a picture of the happy couple with Shawn, the officiant. Then came Beret and finally me.

"Alright. I think I have everything. Did I miss anyone?" she asked.

"Did you get my good side?" asked Beret. "Listen, I don't need to see them. Just tear up the baddies, okay?"

I looked over at Luke watching us pose from the sidelines. I wasn't sure what to do.

"I'd like a picture with Derek and Luke," said Mom, as if she had read my mind.

I glanced her way. "Mom, I…"

"Don't argue with your mother," she said sternly. "Luke, get over here. Aisha, just tell us when you're ready."

Luke walked over and stood on the other side of my mom and smiled.

"Not there," she said. "Other side, with Derek. Where

you belong."

"Mom, we're kind of…"

"Oh, *shoo*. Nothing of the sort."

And that was that.

Sometimes mother knows best.

■■■

"You guys got this?"

I huddled quickly with Sam and Crosby as the last guests slowly shuffled out the door, a bit happier and boozier than they were when they came in. Tucker had already driven Mom and Dad to Parkville's premiere boutique hotel downtown, a small wedding gift courtesy of Barry and me, and now he was chauffeuring a few other guests who were unable to drive themselves. There was a Secret Sunday scheduled for tonight, but even Beret had decided to skip this one.

"I've been in these heels all day," she said. "Right now, I just want a tub of ice cream and the couch. Tucker will be home soon enough with some takeout. You coming?"

While that sounded appealing, I knew I had something more pressing to take care of.

"I'll be along in a bit."

Beret nodded knowingly. "Or you won't. Whatever you

do, just think it through. Try not to coast on the fuel of emotions. Use your head this time. Got it?"

"Got it."

I gave her a kiss on the cheek and turned to see my shadow, never far away. He had barely left my side since he had arrived. I knew he was nervous, but I also understood that the best way to handle all of this was just to talk it out.

"You ready?" I asked.

"Where to?"

"Our place."

■■■

I followed his Jeep to the house in Willie Nelson, my trusty junker of a car. Maybe it would be time to retire him soon, now that I fancied myself a respectable businessman. That was a thought for another day. When I pulled into the driveway everything felt right. I had missed this place, and Luke. But could we really get back on track?

He unlocked the door and placed his keys on the side table. Without even asking he walked over to the bar cart and poured a bourbon for me and then grabbed a beer for himself from the fridge. Ella was already queued up on the stereo as he lifted the arm in place and pressed play.

"Pulling out all the tricks?" I asked, swirling the glass of bourbon in my hand.

"No tricks. Just making you feel comfortable. Or me. I'm not sure. I'm kinda nervous."

"Me, too," I admitted.

He leaned in and tested the waters. The kiss was soft, and I didn't fight it. It felt nice. Good.

"Better?" he asked.

I just smiled, then pulled away and slowly stepped backward to take a seat on the sofa. He joined me, took the drink out my hand and placed it on the table, then reached over and held both of my hands in his.

"I want you to know how sorry I am. Really. *I'm sorry.*" He said the words slowly, with emphasis. "I was dealing with a lot. Fletch was a lot. My past came crashing in and I let myself get swept away. It shouldn't have affected us, but it did, and I let that happen. I assure you, though, my loyalties are to you. They always will be. It's hard for me to explain it. I think I just needed everything to fall apart for me to understand what we had. What we *still* have. I'm kicking myself for how I acted. I was just too stupid to realize how stupid I was."

"You weren't stupid. You were just…"

"*Stupid.* Lost. Blind. I don't know. Pick a word. You're better at that than I am. You know I don't express myself as well as you do. Whatever it was, though, just know that it has passed. The memories, the wild oats, the fears… they're all gone. I know where I'm supposed to be. I just hope you still feel the same."

I took a deep breath. "I'm scared," I confessed. "Not that we won't work out. I'm sure we will. We can, again. I'm just scared of another dark corner and not knowing what will come up. I can't deal with another Fletch. I just can't."

He looked down, then back to me. I felt trapped in his blue eyes. "I get that. I understand. But I promise you, I won't let you down again. I won't let *us* down again. I just want our lives to go back to normal. Our friends, the Firelight, school."

"Evenings with my uncle the drag queen and his twink boyfriend?"

"Exactly." He smiled. "Strippers and martinis and goat cheese pizzas at Chesty Cheese."

"We do have quite the life," I mused.

"We do." He paused, then kissed me softly once again. "Waddya say, babe?"

"There's only one thing left to say." I looked down the hallway. "I hope you didn't try to take more closet space. Because I bought *a lot* of shoes when I was depressed."

"How many is a lot?"

"Remember when we talked about fixing up this place and expanding? When we thought Jett was going to move in with us? I think it's about time we took up that conversation, again."

"Babe, if you want an entire wing for shoes, I'll build it with my own two hands."

Now that, my friends, was the definition of love.

2

MAKING UP IS HARD TO DO

"Did you just tap out?"

Once we started, we didn't stop. We took a few breaks for snacks to replenish our energy, but we had a lot of making up to do and we went for it. Multiple times.

"I'm sorry," I said, out of breath. "I just need a break. You have school in a few hours, and I have work."

"Yes, but I know your boss," he said, nuzzling my neck. "I have a feeling he'll let you off the hook."

"Yeah, but I know *your* boss, and Bammy won't be so

pleased if you leave those kids unsupervised. They tend to act all *Lord of the Flies* when they're left to their own devices, remember?"

"Once a teacher, always a teacher, eh?"

"I just know what those kids are capable of."

"True. But I can get by on three hours of sleep. And there's one more thing I've been meaning to try out. If you trust me, I'll make it worth your while."

He was *not* lying. I've always said that the internet was a great source of knowledge, and believe me, he must have studied hard while we were apart!

I slammed my hands on the bed and clutched at the sheets, the star of my very own fantasy.

"Safe word! Safe word!" I screamed in ecstasy.

He just laughed, and I deserved it. Boy, did I ever deserve it.

···

"Thanks for taking care of everything yesterday, guys. I really appreciate it."

Sam and Crosby were sitting in chairs across from my desk as they recapped the night's events.

"No problem," said Sam. "The wedding was the easy part. Secret Sunday was a handful on its own, though.

Lloyd Barton and Mayor Bellman had a few too many. I don't know what brought it on, but they were cussing up a storm at the bar. We had to ask them to tone it down for everyone else's benefit."

"Hell, they weren't even interested in watching Chip strip," said Crosby. "And you know he's always a crowd pleaser."

"Bellman was spitting nails, yelling about some argument from their past. I was pretty sure he was gonna start throwing punches. But he was so drunk he could barely stand," said Sam. "Crosby had to take him out on the terrace to cool off and drink some water. We had to call Tucker to come drive him home. We knew a regular taxi wouldn't be discrete."

"Thanks for dealing with that, guys. This town has no shortage of drama, that's for sure. I'll come up with some excuse to check in with Lloyd today to make sure everything's okay. Hopefully they got whatever it was out of their systems and they won't be at each other's throats next time they see each other. If not, we can leave the gossip for the *Parkville Post* to unearth. That's none of our business. Now, let's go over this month's schedule."

Not only was the Duke performing well but we were on track to make a profit after just six months of running. Amber's nuclear meltdown of an engagement ceremony had really put our name in the papers and word of mouth had spread like wildfire in our quirky little town. And it didn't hurt that we continued the tradition of catering to the (very closeted) gay elite on the first Sunday of every month, just as Lloyd had. These men had their secrets and even though that was not my style, I understood where they were coming from in this very small town of ours. I was more than happy to oblige them their privacy, as long as they made their deals and gossiped over drinks and appetizers at the Duke. I wondered what had set off Lloyd and Mayor Bellman, though? We were sure to find out soon enough, as nothing stayed secret for too long in this town, that was for sure.

Patience, Derek.

"Listen, Boss, we're pretty shorthanded for the fall," said Sam. "Is it cool if we put out the word that we're hiring bar and service staff? Classes have started so there are plenty of university students looking for some extra work."

"Let me check the numbers and I'll get back to you this week."

The truth was, I knew we could afford to add more waitstaff, but what I really needed was someone to help me run the place. I was trying to wear too many hats at once; owner, office manager, accountant, creative director, and project manager. Luke and I had planned to do this together but that didn't play out as we had discussed. Something needed to give, but I didn't know what. Or who.

■■■

Luke was sitting on the bench by the front door putting his shoes on. We were heading out to the Firelight to meet the Scooby Gang for drinks.

"Hey, pretty boy," I said. I couldn't help myself. No matter how much my mind told me to be angry or worried, my heart reminded me that making up with him wasn't as difficult as I thought it would be.

"Are you looking at your reflection again?" he asked, looking up at me and smiling.

"Yes, in that mirror behind you. How do I look?"

He laughed. "Handsome as always. All that's missing is a drink in your hand."

"That's a simple enough fix. Grab your keys, babe. You're driving."

"Well, that's not unusual."

I looked at him faux seriously. "Not everything has to be a sexual innuendo."

"Since when? Did you change the rules again?"

"I'll make sure to send you an updated manual. Now let's go funnyman!"

I was excited at the thought of seeing everyone as we climbed into the Jeep and sped off. It had been a few weeks since Mom and Dad's wedding, and it was safe to say that we didn't have any regrets in reconciling so far. Getting used to each other again, however, was taking a bit of time. We were trying to make our roads converge again, and little moments from our time apart kept interrupting our newfound groove. Though we were occasionally walking on eggshells, afraid to say the wrong thing or make a wrong move, it was probably just a matter of time before we gelled again with no more glances in the rearview mirror. At least we both hoped so.

"Lips Like Sugar" by Echo and the Bunnymen was playing on the jukebox as Luke and I entered the Firelight for the first time as a couple in several months. This place was our 'bar away from home,' and our friends were right where we left them in the big banquette in the corner.

"*Hello*, elephant!" Kit exclaimed, smiling broadly at Luke. "Welcome to the room. We were *just* talking about you."

"Really, Kit?" I said. "I mean, he has gained a *little* weight since you saw him last, but an elephant?"

"Oh, there will be no discussions about weight," said

Bammy. "If anyone has gained the pounds it's been me. I'm four months along and all I can think about is eating."

"I'm so jealous," said Meredith. "I wish I had an excuse to eat everything I wanted. Maybe a baby would be just the thing?" she teased.

"I feel like I know this drill," said Tommy as he stood up to make his escape. "I'm getting drinks. What can I get for y'all?"

"Something non-alcoholic with lots of bubble water and limes," said Bammy. "And a tiny paper umbrella, if they've got one. Anything to make me *think* I'm drinking. I swear, I cannot sit here and *not* drink. I get so bored. Some things are just too ingrained in my DNA."

"Your mama would be so proud," I said.

"I'll help you, Tommy," Luke offered.

They both walked towards the bar and I took my place next to Kit.

"*Tell. Us. Everything!*" she said. "You have five minutes before they get back. Go!"

"I'm not sure where to start," I said. "It's been good. We've had a few awkward moments, things that were said or done while we weren't speaking, but nothing too complicated to fix. Overall, it's just felt right. We know each other so well that getting back into our rhythm has been pretty easy. But I still have this terrible monster named Fletch occupying way too much space in my head, and I kind of expect him to show up again at any moment. I just don't think we could handle that again."

"Well you have nothing to worry about there," said Bammy. "Remember, I took firing range class in seventh grade, so I can handle a gun."

"Wait, what?" sputtered Michael.

"Gun class. The school board considered that much more important than sex education. And I gotta tell ya, it has definitely come in handy more times than I thought it would."

"You scare me," he said.

"She should," I nodded. "I know things. I'll fill you in later."

"Don't you dare!" she shrieked. "Some secrets need to go quietly into the night."

"I tell ya who hasn't been going quietly into the night," I teased. "Luke has definitely been keeping me up way past my bedtime. We've had a ton of fun getting reacquainted. That man picked up a few tricks from the internet during our hiatus."

"Damn it, Derek? Do I need to go back to the bar to avoid this conversation?" said Tommy as he placed a tray full of drinks on our table.

Luke stood beside him and chuckled. "Watch out,

babe. People are gonna think you like me."

"Oh, they know better."

■■■

We spent the next hour catching each other up on our lives. Luke was serious about renovating our place, so he and Tommy got to work discussing the changes he wanted to make to the house. The plans were to update the bathroom, expand our bedroom a few feet into the back yard, and use the extra square footage to create a walk-in closet for me and all my shoes. Now if that wasn't love, what was?

"A shoe closet!" squealed Meredith. "Between the baby and this, I am getting so inspired by you guys."

"Can you guys stop giving her ideas, please? Luke, this is gonna cost you," said Tommy, shaking his head. "And not because of materials."

"No worries, man. Derek's worth it." His arm gripped me tighter around the waste where it had been since he sat down next to me.

"Speaking of babies," I said. "How are you feeling, Bammy?"

"All is well. Actually, it hasn't been that bad at all. You hear these awful stories about morning sickness and women who are bedridden, but I feel pretty good, to tell you the truth. I'm just ravenous, that's all."

"She's not craving any one thing in particular," said Michael. "It's more like *everything*. Our takeout bill has gone through the roof."

"No lie." She waved her hand. "We have a tab at Cochon's, now. They're just gonna bill us monthly. That baby's gonna come out covered in barbeque sauce."

"With a plaque on the wall at Cochon's for customer of the year!" he said.

"Well, when y'all decide to get married you know who to call," said Kit. "Shawn's officiating business is booming."

"I have you to thank for that, Derek," he offered. "Since your parents' wedding, the phone hasn't stopped ringing. It's been great to pull in some extra bucks on top of the music gigs. It seems there are plenty of folks out there who are into having a non-religious, online-ordained preacher man!"

"Now I'm a band groupie *and* a wedding widow," said Kit. "Shawn's been booked up all over town."

"I love it," he said. "Aisha and I are sending each other work now, too. Her with the photography and me officiating. It's been pretty cool."

"I should have signed you as an exclusive to the

Duke," I said. "Now everyone has a piece of you."

"Well, you'll always be my first," he teased.

"Stop it, honey!" said Kit. "You'll make me jealous, and I can't add possessiveness to the mix right now. I'm already feeling maternal now that Bammy has all of us dreaming of babies."

"Please, no more baby talk," said Tommy, his face in his hands.

Kit took the hint and dove right in, telling us about the upcoming shows and events at the gallery she shared with Meredith. Our little town of Parkville sure had matured over the years since I moved back home. I liked to think that I had had something to do with it, but I couldn't take all the credit. The sparks were here all along. Something (or someone?) just needed to get the fire going. My Uncle Barry did always say that I had an explosive personality. I was just never sure if he meant it in a good way or not.

The evening was coming to a close and we were all just about to go our separate ways when a familiar face showed up at the door, scanned the crowd, and made a beeline right for the edge of our table. She was dressed casually in pastel pink chinos with a cute white cotton blouse that tied in a bow at her waist. A matching pink silk scarf held her blond hair in a high ponytail. The accessories, as always, were diamonds and gold.

"Is there room for one more?" said Luke's sister, Lana.

"Always," he said, as he stood up to give her a hug. She looked over at me from the side of his shoulder and winked.

"Well," I said to her, "if I didn't know any better, I'd think you were getting used to me."

"But you *do* know better, don't you?" she corrected me. "I'm fully aware it was my brother who messed up this time, but if you step out of line like he did, you'd better watch out. This woman knows how to handle a pistol."

"Oooh, I *like* her," said Bammy, perking up.

Lana took a seat next to her brother and then spoke to no one in particular. "Can they make a decent martini in this place or is that asking too much?"

"Oh!" exclaimed Kit. "I like her, *too*! Yes, trust me. I've trained the bartenders with a few thousand martinis over the years."

"That's my cue," said Luke. "I'll be right back." He turned to me. "You want anything?"

"Just you," I said.

"And that's *our* cue," said Tommy.

Don't get me wrong. Tommy loved that Luke and I were in love again, but he was never the mushy talk kind of guy.

"You ready?" he nodded to his girlfriend. "We're

meeting Meredith's parents for an early brunch tomorrow. They have a thing for breakfast foods."

"We should head out too," said Shawn, his arm around Kit. "I have another wedding tomorrow and I need to be fresh."

They kissed their good-byes all around and the four of them headed home.

Luke returned with her drink and Lana took a sip of her martini. She smiled lovingly at her brother. They had had their share of ups and downs, but it was obvious that they didn't just love each other because they were supposed to, but they genuinely liked each other as well.

"How's it going at school, Coach?" she asked him.

"Pretty well. We're gonna have a stellar team this year. No more rebuilding. It's time to let my seniors loose and take Burlington down once and for all."

"That's my Parkville Commodore," I said, admiringly. "No problem students so far?"

"No, not at all. There aren't really any troublemakers anymore now that Chip has graduated, and Jett is off in New York with Fletch..." He stopped before going any further as he realized what he had said. I had never seen him turn so pale so quickly. Before I could reassure him that I was okay, Lana spoke up and beat me to the punch. But what she said shut both of us up, and fast.

"*Now you've done it.*" She placed her drink down dramatically. "You've said it. 'Fletch.' Get that name out of your system for good, brother. 'Cause that asshole has caused enough grief for my friends and family. You, Amber. Even Derek. No more, alright? 'Cause we are *all* over that, no? It is well past time to move on."

She raised her glass and we both did the same. No matter how many times Lana was full of venom for me, she always turned around and offered support when I needed it most. She was full of surprises, that one.

"You know what Mama always told us," she said. "Never go to bed angry. So, if y'all got some unfinished business, you'd better take care of it tonight. 'Cause I am not going through that heartache of watching you two suffer again. You hear me?"

We both nodded and I could feel his strong arm comfort me even harder than before.

"Besides," she added. "I just lose weight when I get upset, and I shouldn't get any smaller than I am right now. I *am* perfect, after all."

"It's okay," I said, ignoring her moment of self-love. "It's just a name. He can't hurt us anymore. We're solid now, right?"

"Definitely," he agreed.

"And besides, I'm sure Jett will be back to regale us

with stories of his new life in New York and Fletch is bound to come up again."

"But for now, let's leave that undesirable topic, shall we?" she said.

"How's the interior design business?" I asked, just as eager as her to move on to other topics. "I read in the *Parkville Post* that you just redecorated the winter pavilion at the country club. Congratulations."

"Thank you. It's good to know that you are at least *attempting* to follow the society pages. I appreciate that you have goals."

And just like that, she was back!

"That project took a lot out of me, but I'm so pleased with the results. To tell you the truth though, I kind of feel like bowing out when I'm at the top of my game."

"Are you thinking of starting something new?" asked Luke.

"I'm not sure yet. I'll take Daddy's advice of course. But nothing's decided. How about you, Derek? I haven't been to the Duke since Amber and Todd's engagement party disaster. Did you ever get all that orange frosting out of the drapes?"

"It wasn't that bad," I said. They both cocked their heads at me, and I had to laugh. "Okay, okay. It *was* that bad. I'll never allow a bride to have orange cupcakes again, even if this is football country. But seriously, business has been great. It's been a lot, actually. Maybe too much. Luke and I had planned on running the Duke together, but since he decided to keep on coaching at the high school, I've really had my hands full. I may have to find someone to help me out."

"Interesting," she said. "Well, I'll see if I can think of anyone." She took another slow sip of her martini and I could actually see the wheels in her head turning.

Oh, Lana. What are you up to this time?

3

LONG LIVE THE QUEEN

"Tucker, what are you doing with your head all the way in the refrigerator?"

"A man has secrets, Barry. A man has secrets."

"Y'all are crazy," I said from the couch. "Are you two always like this? Don't answer that. I already know."

I had decided to spend Sunday with my uncle and his boyfriend. Things were going well with Luke, but I figured a day of distance could only help us more. Besides, he wanted to spend time with his dad, Red, and his stepmom Rosa. I had become increasingly comfortable visiting them at the very impressive Walcott Manor, but I wasn't one hundred percent at ease going back there just yet. After Belle and Lloyd's argument, somehow Red had now gotten involved. I didn't want anything to do with that. There was far less drama at Barry's, right? Oh, who was I kidding?

"Tucker! We just had breakfast, and now you're eating again? You think you're invincible now, but just you wait until that metabolism catches up with you when you get older. Then you'll be surprised."

"Oh, you'll love me no matter what. Don't even pretend," he said as he pulled out a tray of cold cuts and cheese to make a sandwich.

"I'm just firing a warning shot," said Barry. "You may be a skinny Minnie now, but a few more years of those carbs and your ass will eventually look like mine. I just don't want you to take up *all* of my bad habits. A few, sure. But not all of them."

"I know you're not religious," said Tucker, "but you should pray every night that I don't adopt your traits."

"Now that's just mean!"

"See? It's happening already."

I had to snicker. Watching these two was like a live reenactment of the best reality show ever. Just replace the outlandish housewives with an aging drag queen and a twink. Tucker brought his sandwich over and sat next to me on the couch.

"How's business these days?" I asked him.

"Booming," he said in between bites. "Now that everyone has car service apps, we've just piggybacked on top of those. It's made our services really accessible. People have too much money to spend in this town. Sure, they can take a cheaper car to get here or there, but they call us when they want something special. And they always know we can be discrete. I've had to take on more drivers, limousines, town cars, you name it. I've pretty much stopped driving, myself. Now I'm just concentrating on expansion."

"He still escorts me, of course," Barry chimed in. "I feel like I have my own personal driver."

"I'm looking to move into another business," said Tucker. "Hey, did you see that Bottom's Up closed down?"

I told him that I hadn't noticed. When Luke and I were on our hiatus I had pretty much become a shut-in and we always spent most of our free time at the Firelight anyway.

"Does that mean we don't have any gay bars other than Secret Sunday at the Duke and that doesn't even really count?" I asked. "That only meets one night a month."

"Exactly," said Tucker. "And that's not so accessible to the younger gays, let alone the L, B, T, or Qs. No offense."

"None taken. You know I just inherited that event

from Lloyd. He was pretty adamant that I didn't change anything, and it never crossed my mind to make it more inclusive."

"Well, you do have that stripper, Chip," said Barry.

"Yeah, that still feels weird for me, considering he used to be a student of mine."

"Well, that student could definitely teach a class in the art of taking off one's clothes," said Barry admiringly.

"He's straight. He just likes the attention. I'm pretty sure he's picked up a few pointers while spending all his tips at Chesty Cheese. Peaches told me that he's one of her best customers."

"I did some digging down at the county record office," said Tucker. "I bet you'll never guess who owns Bottom's Up?"

"Please tell me it's not Mayor Bellman?" I asked.

"Nope. Lloyd Barton. You think you could help me set up a meeting with him? I think it's time to let the rainbow shine a little brighter. Parkville has changed so much in the last few years and I'd like to do my part for everyone in the LGBTQ community, not just the older gays. The next generation is definitely here. We just have no place to go."

"Except for my hot tub on Saturday nights," said Barry. "You've had a few wild parties here. Trust me, I'm not complaining!"

"Of course, I'll help you," I said. "I've been meaning to talk to Lloyd, anyway. He's not been acting himself lately. This'll give me an excuse."

"Sweet! I appreciate that."

Just then we heard the familiar bells of the ice cream truck through the open windows. Summer was coming to a close, but the warm weather continued in our quaint little town.

"Oh! The ice cream truck!" said Tucker, dropping his sandwich plate on the coffee table in a rush. "I just love the idea of food moving towards me, don't you?"

And with that, he was off and out the door.

"So much energy," I said, shaking my head.

"You would think," said Barry. "But put his head on a pillow and he's out like a light for twelve hours. I've never in my life seen someone who can fall dead asleep in thirty seconds. And then he's like a ragdoll. I just push him and pull him wherever I want."

"Sounds perfect." I smiled.

"It is. He is. *We* are. Who would have thunk it, right? This old queen and her twink in a shiny black limo."

"You deserve all the happiness."

"Yes, I do," he nodded. "I don't feel bad about it at all. But speaking of happiness, how's it going in your reconvened house? How's your head?"

"No complaints," I said, smiling. "It was strange at first how easy it was to get back on track, but what's right is right. I think we've hit all the worst bumps. The universe wants us together so I'm just keeping my eyes looking forward. I'm a greyhound."

"That's the key, Nephew. You can't get stuck in the past. Regrets, mistakes, missteps, they're all part of life. Everything you've done, everyone you've met, every experience you've ever had has led you to who you are at this very moment in your life. It's up to you to decide who you want to be. You're in charge of that, you know?"

"When did you get so philosophical?"

"That one," he pointed out past the window. "Running towards an ice cream truck. He gets it. The rest of us are just thinking too hard."

Just then his phone started humming. He ignored it.

"I think you got an email," I said casually.

"Is that what that is? I can't figure this thing out. Tucker and I went and upgraded my phone last week, but it just confuses the hell out of me. Phones used to be for calls, and now as far as I can tell it's for games, photos, and smiley faces. Swipe left, stare there, press that. The only thing that I want to tap just chose ice cream over me. He tried to explain all the functions, but I just got lost. He spends most of his time playing with SnapCrap or whatever. Most of his messages to me look like they're coming out of a talking pink unicorn."

"Here, let me help you out." I showed him where the mail icon was and tried to explain the difference between an email and a text message. SnapCrap was above my pay grade though, I had to admit.

He reached for his readers on the little table next to his lounger. "It's from Chinois! I got an email from Chinois!" His eyes grew wider the longer he read, until he pulled the specs from his face dramatically. "Nephew, we have work to do. Preparations! Parkville is about to get a visit from New York's very own drag queen extraordinaire, Chinois Zarée!"

■■■

Born as Charlie Zaretsky, Chinois was a mentor and lifelong friend of Barry's. Her message was short and sweet, telling us the when and how, but leaving out all the details of why she wanted to visit. All we knew was that she was coming to stay, and it felt more like a statement than a request. Of course, Barry was thrilled, but I couldn't help but feel a tiny bit apprehensive. I had met Chinois on our last visit to New York. There was nothing subtle about her, and even though our town had expanded its horizons,

I wasn't one hundred percent sure it was ready for a force of nature like Chinois. But Parkville, like Lana, could still surprise me.

"So, she'll stay in your guest room, of course," I said. "But for how long?"

"She doesn't say," said Barry. "She can stay as long as she wants. What do I care?" He put the phone down.

"Well, there's Tucker, for one."

"Oh, he's never anything but friendly to everyone he meets. I'm sure he'll be just fine with it. Besides, Chinois can tell one hell of a story, and Tucker does love his gay history."

"True. And you do have the Bears' Club. I'm sure she'll get a kick out of that."

"We'll put on a show for the members! Oh, Nephew, this is exactly what I needed to get myself up and out again. We haven't had anything exciting happen since your mom's wedding. I have to pull looks, wigs, music. I need a mood board! I have to call her right now. I have so much to do! She'll be here in a week. I'm pretty sure I still have those matching ABBA jumpsuits somewhere. I think they're in that stack of boxes out in the shed, by the weed killer."

Well, of course, they were.

...

Monday morning, I placed a call to Lloyd Barton the old-fashioned way, on the telephone. Lloyd wasn't a text message kind of guy, he liked to do things the old school way. I decided to invite him to a private luncheon at the Duke. I wanted him to see what I had done with the place so that he would understand how much love and attention to detail I had put into it. Even though the project I wanted to discuss with him would not be mine, I figured if he felt I was involved in some way then we wouldn't have any troubles convincing him to sell the Bottom's Up lease to Tucker. Lloyd had a general distrust of people he didn't know so well. While there were so many unknowns in his own past, he was privy to far too many secrets of so many of Parkville's older, closeted generation. I asked Tucker to sit this meeting out. If Lloyd said 'no,' I didn't want him to be too disappointed. Besides, I knew exactly what tricks to pull. Crosby was there to serve and clear, and it didn't hurt that he was easy on the eyes. I wanted to do everything I could to put Lloyd at ease and to help Tucker. After all, he was family now.

Lloyd arrived at 12:00 sharp in his perfectly pressed trademark seersucker suit. Tucker had sent a car for him, of course, on the house. As he walked in the front door of the Duke, I could see his eyes darting about left and right, seeing what had changed, what was new, and what had remained exactly the same.

"I see you've kept the painted clouds on the ceiling, after all," he said as a Mona Lisa smile slowly crept upon his face. You could never quite tell where you stood with Lloyd, and he enjoyed every minute of it.

"Some things are just tradition. And we didn't want to depart too much from what you had established so well."

That was it, Derek. Compliments, compliments.

Crosby appeared at our side in his tuxedo shirt, black bowtie, and trousers with a perfectly polished silver tray balanced on one outstretched hand. "Your vodka stinger, Mr. Barton."

"Why, Crosby, you remembered." The words dripped and drawled from his lips.

"Of course, sir. I've taken the liberty to set up a table on the terrace for your lunch. It's such a lovely day, I thought you gentlemen might enjoy the fresh breeze. Lunch will be served in fifteen minutes. Please, do ring the bell if you require anything of me in the meantime. Anything, at all," he added suggestively with a smile.

It took everything I had not to giggle with pride. Crosby was worth his weight in gold.

"This way, Lloyd," I started. "I'm excited for you to see

the terrace in bloom. Even though it's late summer, we still have a fine garden going."

"Well, you do know that I highly value a well-placed magnolia."

Crosby held the chair out for Lloyd, then excused himself to check on Chef and the luncheon. He knew that Lloyd preferred the kind of server who seemed invisible, appearing only long enough to bring food, clear a plate, or fill a never-ending glass of alcohol.

"This is all lovely, Derek, thank you. It's very nice to be welcomed home to my former haunt. But let's cut to the chase, shall we? We both know there's a reason for this tête-à-tête. I'd just like to know what it is. After all, I do make it my habit to know most everything, but I must admit I have felt a bit out of the loop the last few months. Retirement is not all it's cracked up to be."

Lloyd was all business, for sure. I hadn't expected him to change. I forged ahead, as planned.

"Actually, your retirement is exactly the reason I asked to meet. I was so grateful that you offered to sell your catering company to me, and I hope you're pleased with the results. The Duke has been well received, and quite frankly, I've started to inquire about some other properties out there that may be interesting."

"What exactly did you have in mind?" he asked.

"You know Tucker, yes? Uncle Barry's boyfriend?"

"Why yes, I am familiar with Beret's paramour. He was so kind to send a town car for me today, in fact."

"As you know, he's a bit younger than Beret, of course. And though we have Secret Sundays here at the Duke, it's just not the right kind of environment for that crowd. Now that Bottom's Up has suddenly closed, we wondered if you had any plans for that space?"

Lloyd waited an eternity to respond, as if he was trying to read my mind, while I had no idea what was going on in his. He took another sip of his vodka stinger, then began.

"It seems I didn't cover my tracks as well as I thought. So many shell companies, but I was bound to mix something up as I have begun my divestment. As I mentioned, retirement is not a job for the weak. I simply have too many pieces in my life. Letting this place go was the first step, and the hardest. After that, watching them all fall away one by one has become easier. I must admit, I feel lighter. Bottom's Up was never 'on brand' for me. The queen who ran that place has retired to Gulf Shores, and I was not interested in the slightest in carrying on any further with that concept. Wagon wheel tables and folding metal chairs aren't my thing, as I am sure you are well aware. So, tell me, what do you propose?"

"Not me. Tucker. He took over the car service business

from his grandfather, and it's thriving. He knows how to make a profit, and I trust him. Plus, he has proven himself capable of keeping his fair share of secrets. He'd like to open a new bar, but cater to a younger, hipper crowd. He says Parkville is ready for it, and I tend to feel the same. All we need from you is a 'yes', and we can start negotiations. What do you say, Lloyd?"

He smiled and took a final, slow sip from his cocktail. His hand lazily reached out and rang the silver bell that was placed in the center of the table. Crosby appeared as if out of nowhere.

"Crosby, fetch some bubbles. Derek and I have something to celebrate."

We continued with our lunch, shifting topics to some light gossip here and there. I casually mentioned that his row with Belle at Secret Sunday had caused a few tongues to wag, but he dismissed me quickly.

"Oh, that's just Belle being a bitch," he said dismissively. "Nothing new there."

■■■

I called Tucker as soon as the waiting town car whisked Lloyd away. To say he was thrilled was an understatement.

"Hell, *yeah*!" he exclaimed so loudly that I had to pull

the phone slightly from my ear.

"Don't get too excited yet," I cautioned. "Nothing is real until it's real and you've signed the paperwork. Lloyd may appear smooth, but he can be just as slippery."

"Too late! I'm imagining it already. I can see the whole place in my head. I'm going to put in a little stage for shows, clear out all those nasty wagon wheels, and ban duct tape as a fixer once and for all. I want to make sure it feels welcoming and just plain *kicks ass* at the same time. It won't be one of these fancy artisanal cocktail places, but it won't be a dump, either. This is going to be a place for everybody in the entire community. I want everyone who walks in those doors to feel like they can be whoever they want to be, and we'll treat them with respect.

"Seems like you've planned it all out. Any idea what you're going to call it?"

"I sure do. Get ready, Parkville. Welcome to Gaycare!"

4

GRAND GESTURES

It took just under a week for Lloyd and Tucker to come to terms and file all the paperwork. Tucker had enough money saved from his car service, but Lloyd insisted that I also invest in the endeavor, even if it was a small amount. Tucker was happy to count me in for the ride. The following weekend Tucker, Barry, Tommy, Luke and I met to help start clearing out the old Bottom's Up. Tommy was more than happy to pick up another job. The Walcotts and the Walters sure kept him busy with renovations.

"I can't wait to see all this junk go," Tucker said as we

surveyed the dusty interior.

"I like old stuff," said Barry. "There's a lot of history here."

"If you like old stuff so much then why'd you pick me?"

"Well, I *do* have a fondness for replacement parts."

"I prefer to think of myself as an upgrade. And upgrading is exactly what I plan to do here. Tommy, can I borrow you for a little tour of the crazy in my mind?"

"Careful," said Barry. "You may get trapped there like I did."

Tucker pulled Tommy by the arm and he started with his extensive to-do list. I glanced over to see Barry staring nervously at his phone.

"What's up?" I asked. "You seem a bit edgy."

"Oh, it's just Chinois. She arrives today and it's all I can think about. I told her I'd meet her at the airport, but she said she didn't want to be a bother. At the very least I insisted we send a car to pick her up. She said she would text when she was on her way. I just don't want to miss the message."

"When was the last time you saw her?" Luke asked.

"Oh, it's been years. Decades, even? We lost touch ages ago, before cell phones and email. Derek was kind enough to search her out for me in New York. It's been great getting reacquainted, but I'm a bit nervous about the face to face. What if she doesn't like me when she sees me?"

"That's not even a possibility," I said. "Look at you. You're fabulous! Plus, you have a hot trophy boyfriend."

"*Plus, I have a hot trophy boyfriend,*" he repeated slowly, smiling.

Just then the phone dinged with a message.

"She's here!" said Barry. "Tucker honey, I love you, but I'm out the door. Have fun with the boys! Derek, you're with me. I need your support."

I turned to quickly kiss Luke goodbye just before we raced out to the car.

"Whatever you do, don't let them put in a ball pit."

"No worries about that," he said. "But it looks like the trampoline is a go."

■■■

I hadn't seen Barry this nervous since the Love All benefit at Kit's gallery when he came out on stage as Beret in support of Luke and me. He was racing around his living room, fixing the imaginary this and that.

"How do I look? I don't want to show her Beret yet. I'm not ready. I hope she's happy to just see Barry."

"Hey, calm down. Do you need a cocktail?"

"More like an entire bar cart. I don't know what's gotten into me. I just haven't seen her in so long and so much has changed in our lives."

"You'll be fine," I said in my best calming voice. "Just be you."

"But who am I? Barry? Beret? My pronouns are a mess."

"You're a friend. That's who you are. Just be a friend. Pronouns be damned."

We heard the town car pull up and the driver gave a short toot on the horn. Barry raced to open the door, and there stood Charlie, his bags behind him on the ground. They both looked each other over, sizing one another up. Charlie made the first move and broke the silence.

"Well, *that* bitch aged."

"Looked in a mirror, lately?" asked Barry, not skipping a beat. "Or did they *all* break?"

The cackling that followed must have been heard for miles and miles.

●●●

Their catch-up session was long and intense. Each time I tried to leave to give them their space they pulled me in with more stories of New York and the dawn of the AIDS crisis. It wasn't just sadness, though. Somehow through it all they still managed to find humor in their lives. What struck me most was the shared intimacy in the knowledge of so many who they had loved and lost: an entire generation of artists, dancers, musicians, models, and more who shone bright, left their mark, and then departed far too early.

I was surprised to see Charlie out of drag, but I assumed it would not have been easy to travel as Chinois. Chinois was such a spectacle, with her not-at-all politically correct, faux Asian, three-inch mask of makeup. The first time I met her in Chinatown she was in full drag with a ginormous, shiny black wig that sprouted chopsticks and glowing paper lanterns. She had actual live goldfish swimming in her plastic see-through heels. Chinois was 'extra,' as Tucker would say. Charlie, on the other hand, was diminutive, balding, and most definitely Caucasian. It was almost shocking how small he seemed, as if he could disappear if you looked at him sideways. But then he opened that mouth, and you certainly knew he could take over the room. And that was saying a lot in Barry's presence.

"So, tell me, Charlie," I asked, "what do you prefer? He or her? Charlie or Chinois?"

"That was never my fight," he said. "I had more important things to worry about, like staying alive.

Whatever floats your boat though. I generally go for Charlie/he out of drag and Chinois/she in drag."

"Like me," chimed in Barry.

"But the drag stays in the closet unless I'm getting that money, honey. I don't pull out all the stops just for anyone."

He went on to tell us that he had become more and more disillusioned with New York.

"Every corner is a bank or a boutique hotel now," he said. "What happened to the danger? I kind of miss the fear of getting my ass kicked in six-inch heels. It kept me alive. There's nothing shocking. No drama. Everyone's seen everything there. I want to cause a stir when I enter a room."

"There's no doubt you'll find that here," said Barry. "Parkville is 'rainbow-friendlier' than it used to be, but it's still a conservative place."

The alarm chimed on Charlie's phone and he reached to silence it.

"Derek, can you grab my carry-on from over there? It's AZT cocktail time."

"No problem."

"I'm sure you're tired from your flight," said Barry. "Forgive me for the hour-long interview, I was just so excited to see you. Why don't you freshen up and we can continue this later?"

"Just gimme five," said Charlie. "I could use a bite to eat. I don't suppose you have a Chinatown?"

We didn't. We had something better.

"I know just where to go," I said.

■■■

We had lunch at Saul's Sushi, and we introduced Charlie to Saul and Rachel, the owners. The three of them got along like gangbusters; a group of New York Jews of a certain age misplaced in the South. Saul kept the food coming and Charlie and Barry supplied the stories. Luke messaged me that he was done helping Tucker and Tommy at Gaycare and that he was on his way home. I used that as my excuse to leave.

As I drove Willie Nelson up our street, I saw two cars parked in our driveway. Luke's black Jeep was pulled up front, but there was an older model hunter green Jaguar convertible right behind it.

Who could that be? I wondered.

I parked Willie on the street, walked up the driveway, and peered into the window of the Jag for a clue. Nothing. The front door of the house opened behind me and I spun around quickly, afraid to see Fletch or Jett or even worse.

Could there *be* worse?

"Nice, isn't it?" asked Luke as he stepped out barefoot to greet me.

"Whose is it?" I asked. "Who's here? Because I really don't think I can handle a surprise today."

"Oh, I think you'll like this one." And with that, he tossed me the keys with a smirk.

They landed in my hand and it took me a second to understand.

"Wait. What? Mine?"

"Yours."

"But, why? How?"

"You want me to take it back?" he teased.

"Hell, no!"

I threw my arms around him and gave him a kiss.

"Seriously, explain."

"I picked it up in the spring, just before we left for New York. You'd been complaining that Willie Nelson was on his last legs. Then we had our blow up and it's been sitting at Scooter's repair shop for a few months. I asked him to fix her up a few weeks ago. She used to be Lloyd's. I'm not sure why, but he let me have her for a song. I didn't complain. I just knew she was meant for you."

"You really are trying, aren't you?"

He nodded.

"What are you gonna call her?" he asked.

"I'm not sure yet, but I think she looks like a proper lady."

"What do you say we take Lady out for a spin, then?"

■■■

Lady drove like a dream. First stop to show her off was Mom and Dad's. Audrey and Johnny were still in their (second) honeymoon phase. They invited us to stay for dinner, but Luke had made other plans with Lana at her place. She still wasn't my favorite, but there were certainly worse people in the world. To be honest, I understood her now so much better than when we had first met. She was tricky, but I knew that if I just played nice, she'd be fine. Well, not too nice. Lana enjoyed a little snippiness. In another life she would have made a fabulous gay man.

We had a nice dinner and cocktails on the back terrace of Lana's lake house overlooking the water. The night was warm, but the occasional cool breeze from the water rose up to refresh us.

"It's beautiful," said Luke. "We had so much fun out here as kids."

"We did," she smiled. "I don't think we wore shoes all

summer. We practically lived in our swimsuits."

"And now we have so many shoes that I have to build a special closet just for Derek," he said.

I shot him daggers with my eyes. I'd never win with Lana in the room.

"Well, at least he understands a good investment. And before you say anything," she nodded towards me, "don't expect much more praise than that."

I twisted an imaginary key over my lips, threw it over my shoulder and reached for my drink.

Luke excused himself to go to the bathroom, and Lana and I sat in silence for a bit, watching the night sky.

"I'm glad you forgave him," she said without looking at me. "He was in pain. He's not anymore. You're good for each other. Don't fuck it up."

"Is that advice or a warning?"

"Both."

I understood where she was coming from. "We're good now. We're only moving forward from here on out."

"Do that," she said. "Because if I have to remove the 'reverse' from that fancy new car of yours I will."

I did not doubt her at all.

■■■

The next morning, I followed Luke to the high school

to see Bammy and check in on her. She was in her fifth month now and really showing. She came out from behind her desk and joined me on the couch in her office.

"How are you feeling?" I asked.

"Large. Just large. If I had only one word to describe myself, that'd be it. I tell ya, there is just no way to describe how weird it is to have a tiny being growing inside of you. And even though I can't wait for it to be over, and I sound like I am complaining a lot, I gotta tell ya, I am kinda loving it. I'm making a human. I'm my own Easy-Bake oven! Our sex life has crashed though. Michael doesn't know the first thing to do. It's like he's terrified of everything down there. I keep telling him that he won't poke the baby, no matter what his friends have told him. Lately I've been taking care of myself. A woman can get herself off in thirty-nine seconds. Leave it to a man and there's just no telling. I can't wait all day, ya know?"

That was my Bammy. Taking it all into her own hands, you could say.

"You've come to terms with the Christmas due date?"

"Well, it's not like I have a choice," she said. "I feel sorry for the kid having to share a birthday and a holiday with the rest of the world. You never know what will happen, though. The baby will come when the baby wants to. I can't imagine my kid won't want to make an entrance."

"Will you tell me if it's a boy or a girl? Have you picked any names? I'm dying!"

"No, Michael and I decided against that. We want to be surprised. And there's no way I'm sharing baby names with anyone but him. I don't need anybody's opinion screwing up my choices."

She went on to tell me that they had been having weekly dinners at the Walcott house with Red and Rosa. The grandparents-to-be were excited about the baby, even if they were disappointed that there would not be a wedding until after the birth. Red was more concerned about his standing in society, but Rosa assured him that the times had indeed changed. After all, she herself used to be the housemaid. Even Lana had given in and accepted her as her stepmother. One out-of-wedlock baby wasn't going to cause even the slightest ripple.

"They're so concerned, it kinda tickles me," she said. "Makes me wanna do something crazy, just to see how they'll react. Maybe I can deliver the baby on stage or something."

"We can do it at Gaycare!" I laughed. "Tucker's putting in a stage. He would love that."

I gave her a goodbye kiss on the cheek and made her promise to reach out if she needed anything. On my way out the door I spotted Miss Mabel clicking away on her old metal typewriter.

"Good morning, Miss Mabel. Nice to see some things never change. Is that old typewriter still working for you?"

"It ain't broke, that's for sure," she said. "They keep trying to make me put my words on the computer. I ain't got no love for that grey box. My fingers don't feel right on that thing."

Her glasses were perched at the end of her nose as she hovered mere inches away from where the typewriter keys slammed against the white page. I was afraid the chain from her glasses would get caught up in the contraption and pull her in. If I had to a place a bet though I'd say that Miss Mabel could take on anyone or anything.

"How's Miss Addie?" I asked. Mabel's sister worked as a housekeeper for Luke's ex, Amber.

"She doin' good. Good as can be. That Miss Amber's one handful, though, I tell you. Even with Jett gone in New York, she's got Addie keepin' busy. Not sure she'll last much longer there. Addie's thinkin' of retirement, soon. Plannin' on taking it easy."

"How about you? What are your plans?"

She stopped typing and sat back in her chair. Looked over her shoulder and then refilled the coffee cup in front of her from the small silver flask buried in the back of her top desk drawer. More and more she'd given up hiding her tippling in the last year. As long as it didn't affect her work, Bammy tolerated it. Miss Mabel was an institution at Parkville High.

"Me? I'll probably die hunched over this desk. I got work to do," she said, with a mixture of dismissiveness and love. "Now git."

...

Miss Mabel must have inspired me. Even though Willie was on his last legs he still had a bit of life left and it didn't feel right to retire him for good. I started him up for one last drive. Luke followed me in the Jeep, and we headed over to Barry's house. Since Charlie arrived, he and Barry had talked about the future. New York was definitely in his past, and it turned out that he had decided to leave it for good. Barry was shocked, but also excited to see what would happen next. Charlie was now a Parkville resident for the time being, or at least until something more exciting came along. And in even better news, Saul hired Chinois to be a waitress at Saul's Sushi. Parkville was getting her first full-time drag waitress. *She got the money, honey!*

As a welcoming gift we offered up Willie and handed

over the keys to Charlie. I was happy to see him getting a new lease on life. Both Willie and Charlie.

Luke dropped me off at the Duke and promised to pick me up after school in my new car. As I walked up the steps and entered the foyer, the phone in my pocket rang.

"Hey, it's Lana. I've found the perfect person to help you out at the Duke. Got a minute? Even better, I'm on my way. You *do* keep your gin chilled, don't you?"

5

THE LADIES WHO LUNCH

"Listen," she started, "I don't want to hear a word from you until I'm done, okay? Nod if you understand."

She entered the Duke like the Hurricane Lana that I knew her to be. She wore a powder cream jumpsuit with a plunging neckline, accessorized with gold Tiffany jewelry and enormous diamond earrings. She placed her Céline bag on the bar before moving to the center of the room, her hands placed powerfully on her hips in a Wonder Woman pose. She didn't come to play. She came to work. Literally.

"You! What's your name?"

Crosby had just entered from the back, his hands full of fresh linens. He stood there frozen, unsure of what was happening.

"Uh, Crosby?" he answered timidly.

"Dry gin martini, extremely chilled, stirred not shaken, straight up, lemon twist. Go!"

His eyes darted to me for reassurance and I nodded my silent approval. It felt like an eternity as he sped over to the bar to complete her order, stirring (not shaking) as she had requested. He quickly carried the perfect gin martini over on a polished silver tray and handed it to her, remaining by her side to gauge her approval.

She took one sip, then allowed her eyes to close and linger in her happy place, perhaps momentarily forgetting why she had stormed the Duke in the first place. Then she quickly rebooted, and her eyes popped open with a renewed focus.

"Good. Now out. We need the room."

And he was gone.

"Lana, I…"

"I've been thinking about something and I need to share," she started, clearly intent on continuing without allowing me to say a word. "As you know, I've run a successful business for years. I'm a one woman show, and I like it that way. My clients do too. They know what to expect when they hire Lana Walcott Custom Interiors. They require a certain level of expertise and I present a clear vision, at an elevated price, of course. The Walcott name brings a certain cachet to the project. It opens doors. Nice doors. Expensive doors. Over the years I've met every socialite in this town. I've redrawn drawing rooms and I've lounged in their lounges after countless remodels. Money is fun, but with too much money comes boredom. When they get bored, they redecorate. And I benefit from that. Trust me, I have overseen every redecoration imaginable except perhaps a moat, and I'm not sure how much longer I can dissuade Chintz Fitzgerald from actually going through with that one."

She took a healthy sip from her martini, strongly aware of the need to consume it before it reached room temperature.

"Simply put, I get shit done and I make it look pretty. But I'm tired of it." She wrinkled her nose. "I need a change. I'm looking for something more, a new creative outlet, something that can get me fired up like I've not been in years. Luke has his coaching, Daddy has his real estate business, and you have this, the Duke. And I want in." She finished the remainder of her martini in one fierce gulp.

Was this my cue?

"Lana, I…"

"Not finished. Listen, I know you and I have not always walked the same path together. Yes, that's an understatement and I don't need the peanut gallery in your mind to say anything out loud right now. I've been tough. But you know me. I am loyal to a fault, even if that fault is faulty. I've made mistakes, sure. Missteps. But who hasn't? You can't say I haven't learned from them. I accepted Rosa as Daddy's wife. I welcomed Michael as my half-brother. I love Luke with all my heart, and I know how much he loves you and that makes me happy. Maybe I don't express that well, but it does. I want love too, someday, and I hope I'll find it, but for now, all I have is my work, and it's unfulfilling. Combining our services together is a no-brainer. Here's what I can bring: full, unfettered access to every rich, bored housewife in this town, a perfect eye for exactly what they want and are willing to handsomely pay for, and the name to help you raise those prices just enough to make an even greater profit than you already do. Will we butt heads? Absolutely. Will we want to strangle each other? You bet. But will we make magic and money and just enough mayhem to keep us both interested in this for years to come? I'm counting on it." She raised her chin and her glass. "To us?"

Oh, now it was my turn?

"That's empty," I said, raising my eyebrows.

"Well, that's why we have Crosby, now isn't it?"

■■■

This was a week of moving and shaking and my head felt like a spinning top. Lloyd divesting cars and businesses, Chinois coming to town and taking a job at Saul's, Tucker planning to open Gaycare, and now me joining forces with Lana. Love makes for strange bedfellows, indeed. But before we could get into business together officially, I had to come clean about who was really *in* the bed. I had no choice but to tell her about Secret Sundays. To her credit, she took it in stride.

"So, you're telling me that there is a secret cabal of closeted gay businessmen who meet here once a month to make deals, eat cheeseballs, and watch a stripper named Chip fulfill their straight boy fantasies?"

"Pretty much."

"Derek, this is Parkville. If there *wasn't* a secret businessmen's club, closeted or otherwise, I would be surprised. Besides, this only strengthens my argument. You have access to the husbands, and I have the wives. I'd say we're pretty much unstoppable."

Lana knew each of the ladies who lunched at the

country club on a very personal level. She knew their ins and outs, their private and public faces. We agreed that she would become the face of the Duke and I would run the goings on behind the scenes. That was fine by me. I had spent years yearning for the stage, and now I was prepared to let someone else take the spotlight. I was maturing, alright? It felt like she had barely come onboard when she began to book event after event, including an engagement party for Lavender Hastings and a divorce celebration for the Fieldings, in which both parties planned to attend. They wanted one final blowout together. She coerced Poppy and Chintz Fitzgerald into throwing a medieval fantasy party for no other reason than to get his mind off the damned moat that she wouldn't allow him to put on his property. And to my ultimate surprise, she even convinced Amber Winthrop to marry Todd Carmichael right here at the Duke, the site of their infamous engagement party.

"You have to take back that memory. Reclaim the space for something happy," she told them. It was a real Oprah moment and it worked. The armchair therapists of the world would have been so proud of her.

■■■

"She's something, isn't she?" Crosby said to me a few weeks later, his eyes following Lana's ass out the door as she left for another appointment at the country club. He stood behind the bar polishing glasses, and from the look on his face I was grateful I couldn't see below his waist.

"Don't shit where you eat, Crosby. Best advice I could ever give you."

"I'd say she's worth losing a job over."

"You're out of your league, pal."

"He sure is," said Sam as he entered from the terrace, his white t-shirt clinging to his chest with sweat. The garden was transitioning from summer to fall and Sam was doing his best to maintain the beauty. We still had several outdoor events coming up. "Any fool can see that she only has eyes for me."

"Shut your mouth," said Crosby. "You're full of it. She hasn't given you the time of day."

"You shut up," Sam countered. "You don't know what you're talking about."

"Both of you shut up!" I raised my voice. "You're *both* beautiful. Now back to your corners. And if I catch either one of you letting the business down because you're letting your pants rule your brain, then you're out of here, understand?"

"Yes, sir," they mumbled in unison and went back to

their work.

I knew I was getting older, but I didn't expect to be a daddy so soon in life. To tell you the truth, it was kind of fun being the boss. Lana sure was right about one thing, though. She was bringing in the magic, the money, *and* the mayhem.

∎∎∎

Amber and Todd's wedding date approached sooner than I could have imagined. I think in some way I had tried to ignore it. It would have been a lie to say that the very thought of it didn't make me feel uneasy. Thankfully, Lana dissuaded Amber from 'reclaiming' her love of orange frosted cupcakes.

I had the day off before the wedding, so I used that time wisely by spending it with Luke. Tommy had finished all the renovations at our place, and I was in heaven. The bedroom was larger, the new bathroom looked like it could have been featured in a magazine, and my expanded walk-in closet was the dream of every Carrie wannabe who ever obsessed over sex, the city, and a great pair of Gucci loafers. Luke and I had just put the new dual showerhead to good use and were now relaxing on the back porch, enjoying a beer, a bourbon, and a soundtrack of crickets.

"Y'all back here?" The voice came from around the corner and we turned to see who it was.

"Jett," I said, flatly.

"Now don't sound too excited," he smirked. "I rang the bell but there was no answer. No bell even."

"Yeah, I never fixed that. We kind of like our peace and quiet," said Luke.

Jett stepped up onto the deck and stood there for a minute before extending his hand to Luke and then me. Was this just for show? One never knew with this troublemaker. He had changed, at least outwardly. He seemed taller than when he had left, though it had only been a few months. He had switched out his sporty look for something more preppy, featuring just the right logos and not too many to appear tacky. His attire looked expensive, but not so showy that it was inaccessible. His hair was trimmed and in place and there seemed to be a new maturity in his eyes. It wasn't sadness. It was more like he had seen things, experienced things, and made it through with new scars to guide him. His smile, though, was just as wicked as ever.

"Surprise! Y'all got a beer for me?"

"In the fridge," said Luke, nodding towards the house.

"He's not twenty-one yet," I reminded both of them.

"I live with Fletch," he said. 'You think I ain't seen and

done things?"

I couldn't argue with him there.

Jett went to retrieve a bottle from the kitchen, and I shot Luke a wary glance. He just shrugged his shoulders as if to say, *Let's see what happens.*

Jett returned with a bottle in his hand, pulled up a chair, and swung his legs out in front of him. "Mama's marrying Todd tomorrow. I can't keep track of how many daddies I've had at this point. They're all out celebrating right now but I don't want any part of that. Trust me, living with Fletch has made partying a whole helluva lot less attractive." He took a swig from his beer then started absentmindedly peeling at the label with his fingers. "Spring and summer in New York were pretty cool, thanks for asking." The kid still had his charms. "I spent the first few weeks fucking up, just like you warned me not to. Fletch made that easy enough. His idea of parenting is a credit card and a key to the front door. It didn't take me long to make friends, and even less to realize they all sucked. You told me before I left that New York was a town made for reinvention. I didn't want to be the same old Jett anymore, so I set out to change that. Not sure if y'all noticed, but I used to be pretty sneaky, for all the wrong reasons." He laughed to himself. "The divorce from Brandee pretty much wiped Fletch out, but big pharma still pays him damn well. He's great at his job but shit at keeping track of his money. It's amazing what you can learn online these days: stock trades, asset management, money transfers. I may suck at French, but it turns out I have a head for numbers. If I told ya about the accounts in Panama though, I'd have to kill ya." He took another sip. "I'm doing pretty well in school, even. Now don't get too excited. I'm not hanging out with the nerds. But I'm avoiding trouble, that's for sure. The guidance counselor says I even have a shot of getting into a decent college, if I really apply myself. I'm staying pretty clean, setting myself up for the future. I can't rely on Amber or Fletch or anyone else, 'cept maybe you two. Whether you like it or not, I'll keep coming back because I know you'll tell it like it is. I need that. I'm serious. No one in my life gives me feedback or praise. I guess I'm kinda asking for you to tell me I've done good." He leaned forward and looked at us earnestly.

"Done *well*," I corrected him.

"Now there's the asshole I know and love," he laughed.

Luke glanced at me and shook his head. "You *have* done well," he told him. "I'm proud of you. We didn't know what to expect from you, but we always knew you were a smart kid."

"Just misdirected," I mumbled.

"Sure," Luke agreed. "He may have been misdirected, but he's turned out alright. We all have. Now we're just counting on you to keep on keepin' on."

Luke stood up and held his arms out. Jett stood, smiled, and threw himself right in. I knew firsthand that feeling of my boyfriend surrounding me with those sturdy biceps, and I didn't want to deprive Jett of that love, even if I still thought he had been a little shit in his younger days. He seemed changed for the better.

"Alright, alright," Jett said, pulling back from Luke. "Enough with the gay shit. They told us all about your recruitment methods in Sunday school."

"Get the fuck out of here," I said, with love. He understood my humor and smiled. "We'll see you at the wedding tomorrow, okay?"

"You can bet on that." He winked at us and placed his beer down on the table. "Alright, I'm off to meet Chip. He's all excited about some chick he's banging, and he can't stop talking about her. Later!"

"Get off my lawn!" I yelled as he walked around the corner of the house.

"Come on," said Luke. "That wasn't so bad. I think he really likes us."

"I know, I'm just messing with him."

It did feel good, actually. The people in this town never

failed to surprise me.

...

Amber and Todd's wedding was, thankfully, uneventful. Jett walked his mom down the aisle, and everyone in attendance seemed to have a great time. In lieu of orange cupcakes Lana had ordered orange beer koozies with the bride and groom's names printed on them in puffy paint. They were a hit and we were grateful that none of them were used as weapons. There were no punches thrown, no drinks splashed in angry faces, and no unexpected trysts in the wardrobe. When the guests started line dancing on the main floor, Lana and I took the opportunity to step out onto the terrace for a glass of bubbles.

"Looks like we'll make it," she said as we toasted to this seemingly unimaginable partnership. I could see Sam hovering in the distance, and I sensed that Crosby wished he were anywhere closer than behind the bar in the main salon. They were still tripping over themselves to see who could impress her the most. It was obvious to me that she was aware of their extra attention but recognizing their efforts would have taken all the fun out of it. She knew what she was doing, and she took advantage of it. Who could blame her? If I didn't already have a man, I wouldn't have minded two hot young guys lusting after me.

"You got this?" The party had started to wind down and she looked beat. It was not easy catering to Amber's every wish. "I think I'm ready to get out of here."

"All taken care of," I nodded.

She handed me her champagne flute and walked out the back towards the parking lot. I started clearing dirty glasses when I heard a voice behind me.

"What's up?"

"Hey, Chip." He seemed both out of place and in the right place at the same time. "It's not Sunday, what are you doing here?"

"Yeah, I know. I came to pick up Jett. We're gonna hang after this is done with. You mind if I buy a few bottles off Crosby?"

"You know where he is," I said, getting back to my dirty glassware. "Just don't do anything stupid."

"Aw, you know me, man," and he turned to walk towards the bar.

Yeah, I did. That's why I said it.

6

THIS TOO SHALL PASS

Gaycare was all set to open on Friday night and Tucker was more nervous than I had ever seen him. We were gathered inside the bar checking all the last-minute details before we opened the door.

"What if they hate it? What if it's all wrong? What if no one shows up?"

"You put notices in every truck stop restroom from here to Kentucky," teased Beret. "One more shout out on Huntr and I'm afraid you'll run out of booze."

"Well I certainly will if your friends show up."

"Hey, remember that summer party you threw at the

Swimming Ho?" I reminded him.

The old rock quarry had been flooded and used as a swimming hole for ages. The locals swam there all summer long. Tucker had decided to 'test the waters,' so to speak, and throw an LGBTQ friendly picnic. He rebranded the place the Swimming Ho and invited all his friends.

"You had so many people show up that the cops had to come and shut it down," I said.

"They just freaked out over the nudity," he answered. "I don't understand all the fuss about not wearing a swimsuit. Most people have seen a penis."

I couldn't argue with him there.

To avoid any unnecessary law enforcement this time around Tucker came up with the brilliant idea of a membership card for Gaycare. As a private club, only members could gain entrance, allowing everyone to enjoy the freewheeling atmosphere he envisioned without any police interference. There were no requirements for membership other than showing up and requesting it. A ten-dollar recurring monthly fee included entrance to the club, one free drink a week, and a fancy digital membership app that Tucker designed. Not only was he guaranteed monthly income, but he could track who frequented his bar, what they drank, and how much each customer spent. Plus, the free weekly drink ensured return visits. His big data could lead to big profits.

"This app is smart," I said. "Maybe we could do something like this for Secret Sundays?"

"I think you are way overestimating the abilities of those old queens," laughed Beret. "They're more likely to understand a stone tablet and a chisel."

"He's not wrong," said Luke. "The last time I went there someone asked me for my business card. When I said I didn't have one, he suggested that our secretaries set up a lunch."

"That doesn't mean anything," I said. "I have a business card."

"Exactly my point," Beret chimed in. "You appeal to your clients, and Tucker has to appeal to his. It's all good. There's room for everyone. I'm just lucky enough to straddle both worlds."

"Is 'both worlds' your pet name for Tucker?" I asked.

"And another fairy gets his wings!" laughed Tucker. "Come on, first round is on me."

I took a look around the bar and admired what Tucker had accomplished. Beret had described Bottom's Up as a 'sad hellhole where gays go to die.' Luke and I had only been there twice together, and I couldn't remember the last time anyone said that they had fun there. Sure, the drinks were cheap, but that's about all it had going for it.

Parkville deserved an upgrade, and Tucker over delivered. Gaycare was not sad in the slightest. It was definitely the 'kick ass place' that he had envisioned. It reminded me of the trendy new spots in Hell's Kitchen that were anything but the typical, outdated gay bars of the past. The interior featured an elevated style, with comfortable, elegant seating areas, a wraparound bar, and a small semicircular stage in the corner, perfect for Beret's inaugural performance.

"Are you nervous?" I asked her.

"Nervous? No, not really. Not for me. I just want Tucker to succeed. I'm happy for him."

"What're you doing tonight?"

"Oh, it's perfect, Nephew. He really had a vison of what he wanted. I'm lip syncing to a few old Edith Piaf songs, just to set the mood before the DJ starts. 'La Vie en Rose' and all that. Very artsy fartsy."

"That explains the pencil-thin eyebrows and the veil," I said. "At first I thought I was getting a Judy vibe."

"Funny you should say that! Chinois and I are planning a Judy and Barbra duet for the Bears' Club next week. It's our big Fall Ball fundraiser. I hope you'll be there?"

"With bells on!"

"Oh, no, that won't do," he teased. "I don't want any competition."

"Where is Chinois, by the way? How is she adjusting to life in Parkville?"

"She's home tonight taking it easy. She's a powerhouse for sure, but her debut at Saul's has taken all of us by surprise. We weren't sure what to expect. One of the older waitresses quit in protest, but I think she'll regret that soon enough. Business is booming, and Saul could not be more pleased. Everyone in town wants to come and see the new (old) drag queen waitress. There's a line out front, if you can believe that. Who would have thought that a snarky old queen could add to the revitalization of downtown?"

"No regrets so far?"

"Regrets? No. It just all went so quickly. 'Here I am, can I move in?' Don't get me wrong, I'm happy she's here. But I'm still not sure why. Why here? Why me?"

"Maybe she just needed a friendly face," I offered. "When I met her in Chinatown she seemed so beaten down. You had spoken so highly of her and I didn't want to disappoint you with her lack of success."

"Well she's certainly found success here. Maybe that's a springboard to bigger and better things? She deserves it. I'm such a fan. Oh! I think it's time."

The DJ started a set of upbeat hits as Tucker walked to the door, ready to open up his exciting world to its new members. The windows were covered in gauzy curtains to shield the prying eyes from the goings-on within, but we had a good idea of what to expect. The throngs poured in and the champagne corks started popping! Gaycare was a rousing success, as we all knew it would be.

Peaches, the owner of Chesty Cheese, was one of the first through the door, and it looked like every exotic dancer who wasn't working a pole that night came with her. "This is fabulous," she exclaimed, air kisses flying left and right. "I know where I'm heading on my free nights now! Girls, to the bar. Mama's buying bubbles."

Later in the evening after Tucker had thanked everyone for coming and supporting the bar, he introduced Beret. She took her place on the stage as the first bars of Edith Piaf started and the crowd grew silent. I was sitting with Luke, our fingers intertwined. He held me close and held me fast. I wasn't seeing life through rose colored glasses. I was living the life I had created.

■■■

"I'm so excited about Fall Ball tonight," I said to Luke as we were getting ready. It was billed as a 'semi-formal' event, but for the Bears' Club members that meant a very specific thing; formal up top and informal below the waist. We both wore white, starched tuxedo shirts, black bowties, tuxedo jackets… and boxer shorts. We even took the extra step and found sock garters to round out the look.

"How is it we can attend this thing?" he asked. "We're not exactly members. Isn't this place supposed to be even more secret than Secret Sundays?"

"Yes, but it's a fundraiser tonight. Members are allowed to bring two guests who can keep their mouths shut."

"And Barry chose us? I mean, *me* sure… but you?"

"Cute. You'd be surprised how many secrets I can keep, *Cowboy*."

He smiled as he adjusted his bowtie in the mirror. "Ah, the old days. Now we're just an old married couple. Well, not married. And definitely not old. Just… I mean. Whatever. You know what I mean."

I chuckled. It was cute listening to him get flustered.

"Come on, let's go. I'm looking forward to seeing Chinois perform. It's her Parkville debut, if you don't count her waitressing job. You mind if I drive?"

"You could use the practice," he winked. "I love you, you know."

"I love you more."

"It's not a competition."

"Good. Then you won't mind me winning."

■■■

I was used to visiting Beret at the Bears' Club via the staff door at the back, so it was nice to enter through the front like an upstanding citizen. I loved the speakeasy window that slid open to check out our identities and the dark wood paneled entry that led to the wardrobe. We checked our coats with the handsome young attendant, our bare legs adjusting to the cooler temperature inside. This place was so different than Secret Sunday at the Duke and I tried my best to take it all in. Who knew when I'd get another chance to visit? Whereas Secret Sunday was a gathering for the closeted, older businessmen of Parkville to socialize, this vaudevillian den was a place for all the open-minded gentleman, both gay and straight, to enjoy a fine whiskey and a laugh. There once was a time when drag was comedy, performed as a joke by straight men like Milton Berle. There was no gender illusion involved, they were physical comedians with fake, lumpy breasts, smeared lipstick, and ill-fitting heels. Cross-dressing was for laughs, not for love. It bothered me to support that notion, and I could understand why Tucker was not unhappy about skipping out tonight. This was not a place to discuss the rainbow that most of us were fighting for today. Rather, I was here to support Beret, so I focused on the fun in that.

"It's a who's who of who not to piss off, isn't it?" I said

to Luke as we scanned the crowd. Lloyd Barton held court at a table with Luke's dad, Red, and they both nodded in our direction as we waved a pleasant hello. Mayor Bellman was in drag as his alter ego, Belle. She hovered over their table, smoking a cigar and laughing along with the jokes I was grateful not to hear. We spotted the head of the city council, a few lawyers, and even some retired military veterans. You haven't lived until you've seen 'semi-formal,' the Army way. Stars up top and striped boxer shorts below.

"I think I'll join my father for a bit, if that's alright?" asked Luke.

"I'll look for Beret. I'm dying to see what she and Chinois have put together."

I made my way to the corner of the proscenium stage, walked up the steps, and pushed my way past the heavy red velvet curtain to backstage.

"Well, happy days are here again," I cried out as Beret and Chinois turned to face me. Beret was the perfect Judy Garland in her shimmery, tuxedo-bibbed jumpsuit. Chinois, in the young Barbra Streisand role, wore a satin sailor suit and shoulder length bob. The nose was hers. They were set to perform a duet of *Get Happy/Happy Days are Here Again* that the stars had performed back on the Judy Garland Show in 1963, a classic if there ever was one.

"This is amazing. The crowd will eat you up!" I gasped.

"They'd better," said Beret. "We've been rehearsing all week. Tucker says we're going to 'slay,' which I'm pretty sure is good thing."

"Barbra and I once had the same manicurist, so I feel a very special connection to her," said Chinois, very seriously.

"And I once had a cat named Liza," deadpanned Beret. "Speaking of cats, look who just dragged herself in off the streets. Who are you supposed to be? The chimney sweep from *Mary Poppins*?"

Belle walked towards the ladies, one hand on her hip, the other holding a bowler hat. "I heard you were performing as Judy, so I thought it was only appropriate I play your daughter, since you are older, after all. I'm Liza from *Cabaret*, bitch."

Oh, the shade was flying tonight! May the best woman win.

"I'm stepping out before you ladies start snatching wigs," I said. "Break a leg, y'all!"

I rejoined Luke and we took our place at a small table for two. We were both really looking forward to the big showdown. Beret and Chinois performed first, and they staged their number completely for comedy, with an endless array of illuminated cardboard arrows that descended from above and pointed directly at 'Judy,' so that the audience would not get confused as to who was the star of the show. 'Barbra' did her best to upstage the master, but at the end of the gay (you read that right), Beret's 'Judy' reigned supreme.

Belle was up next, and to my surprise, she went the drama route, rather than comedy. She had proven herself a fan of torch songs and tonight she picked a real doozy. She staged 'Maybe This Time' at a powder room table, her face peering through the frame where the imaginary mirror was placed so we were privy to every nuanced pang of love, lost and longed for. As the crescendo built to the end, she raised one fist mightily in the air and sang defiantly, 'Maybe this time, I'll win,' then bowed her head as it fell to rest on the table. It was a tour de force, and even I surprised myself when I jumped to my feet to join the thunderous applause.

"She's really milking this, isn't she?" said Luke as he clapped away.

Belle had yet to raise her head, her body slumped over the tabletop. The applause continued and she still kept her pose.

"She's not *that* committed," I said, slowing my hands down. "*I think she's dead.*"

■■■

In the first moments after her performance no one had realized she had passed on. But when the applause died down and she hadn't moved, it was Beret who stepped out onto the stage to check on her frenemy, Belle. Sure, they had been catty with each other, but the friendship they had was undeniable. A doctor in the audience quickly jumped on stage and made an assessment. Belle was gone, and no 911 call, ambulance, or emergency technician could save her. What they could save, however, was her legacy.

Parkville had developed a habit of cycling through its mayors in the most undignified of ways. Mayor Tazewell had passed in the champagne room at Chesty Cheese and now Mayor Bellman had expired on the stage at the Bears' Club in full drag. Tazewell caused a mini scandal, but Red was determined that Bellman's death should transpire with dignity.

"What exactly are you saying, Red?" asked Lloyd as the crowd had finally calmed down enough to listen. "Are you saying we should move him?"

"Yes, I think we should. We have to," he said. "Edward would do the same for any one of us. His wife Bitsy will have it hard enough; do we really need to add all of this glamour to the mix? He enjoyed his life here as

Belle, but these are private gatherings, and those moments were intended for us, and for us only."

"I don't know what you're playing at here, but I will have no part of this," said Lloyd. "The Glama Gals were disbanded years ago. We owe each other nothing. This travesty will neither make up for the past nor put a positive shine on anyone's reputation." He turned solemnly to leave. Several gentlemen followed, but a surprising number remained.

My ears perked at the mention of the Glama Gals. That was the second time I'd heard that, the first being when our blended families shared a few drinks at the airport this past spring. But before I could dwell on it, Luke spoke up.

"I'll help you," he said.

I practically jumped out of my skin. "What? We can't get involved in this. Are you crazy?"

"I have to help my father. He needs me right now. If you need to go, I understand."

"And miss this shit show? Not on your life."

What happened next was something that I will never forget. The men descended on Belle like the children on Montgomery Clift at the end of 'Suddenly, Last Summer.' They pulled at his clothes, removed the wig, and wiped his face clean of all the makeup and false lashes. They dressed him back in his suit, then lay him gently on the stage floor.

"What do we do now?" I asked. "Are we supposed to 'Weekend at Bernie's' him to his house? We can't roll him up in a rug."

"I have an idea," said Beret.

Have you ever tried to fit a six-foot-tall dead man into a garment bag intended for a wedding dress? *I can only hope your answer is 'no.'*

Luke lifted him over his shoulder and carried the body solemnly through the backdoor employee entrance. Well, he did it as solemnly as he could. The bag did have 'Irma's Bridal' printed on it after all.

"Good thing I drove Lady," I said. I popped the doors open and Beret helped me pull down the soft top of the convertible. Luke placed the garment bag in the back seat as gently as he could.

"You're a good man, son," said Red. "I appreciate this."

Luke nodded, then closed the door to the passenger seat. I pulled out of the parking lot and started towards our destination.

"Back roads?" I asked.

"Back roads, for sure."

We arrived at Bellman's house and I killed the lights as we pulled up to the side of the house. Red had told us that the bedroom was upstairs, but other than that, we had no plan.

"I can't believe we're doing this," I said. "This is insane. Who are we protecting here? Bellman, or the Bears' Club?"

"My father," he said. "We're doing it for Red."

"How do you plan for us to get in there?"

"You're not. I am. Stay here. I don't want you involved in this anymore than you have to be."

He jumped out of the car, lifted the garment bag over his shoulder, then ran towards the side of the house, still clad in a tuxedo shirt and boxer shorts. He was quite the sight. An ivy-covered iron trellis led to the second floor, and I can't imagine anyone but Luke could have carried the full weight of another man up the side of the house as he did. He reached the top and thankfully the window slid right open. He was inside for only a few minutes when suddenly a light switched on at the other end of the house.

"Get out of there, Luke. Fast!"

Suddenly I saw him appear at the open window and throw the empty garment bag out onto the lawn. He practically ran down the trellis, swooping up the bag as he raced towards the waiting car. He was barely inside when I sped off, only turning my lights on as we entered the main road. My heart was racing, and my body was filled with adrenaline.

"Oh my god. Oh my god, oh my god, *oh my god*. What did you do? Where did you put him?"

"I had to think fast. The light came on as I entered the hall, so I knew I didn't have much time. I pulled him out, pulled his pants down, and sat him on the toilet."

So much for dying with dignity!

7

I HEAR YOU CALLING

We barely slept through the night. No doubt the adrenaline racing through us had something to do with that. I imagined that every sound I heard was the cops coming to get us. Eventually we both passed out from exhaustion. Right before we went to New York I had had a fever dream in which Belle appeared to me in her favorite Carmen Miranda outfit. I kind of wanted to have that dream again so I could take charge of it and confirm that we did the right thing. I wanted to talk to her. I needed to know that she was happy with our choices, but we would never know that. At least Bitsy Bellman would not have to publicly accept her deceased husband's crossdressing passion, on top of her already unimaginable grief, and that eased my mind, ever so slightly.

"Morning," I said to Luke as I gave up staring at the wall and turned over to face him. I could practically hear him thinking. He had tossed and turned all night. "Are you okay?"

"As well as I can be," he sighed. "There's no going back, that's for sure. I just hope we did the right thing."

"Only time will tell. Let's grab the paper and see if there's any news."

We slipped out of bed, threw on our house clothes, and walked down the hall hand in hand. My phone rang before we could reach the front door.

"Did you see the paper?" said Barry without even saying hello.

"Not yet. Luke's getting it now." I nodded for him to retrieve it as I sat on the couch.

"Everything's fine. He's the headline, of course, but there's nothing to suggest anything untoward. We did the right thing."

I hoped so. Because the last thing I needed was something else biting me in the ass. I had seen enough action in this town already. Barry and I talked for a few minutes more while Luke pulled the eggs from the fridge and started breakfast. The Bears' Club members and the invited guests who had remained had all been sworn to secrecy, and he intended to abide by that. Tucker would never know what happened last night. We all agreed to just move on with our lives and pay our respects when the time came. After all, this wasn't the only town secret, and it wasn't even the worst. Barry went on to say that Gaycare had a great opening weekend. Tucker had messaged him that he closed down the bar and stayed at his own place last night, so there wasn't even an opportunity to notice that something was off with Barry. As for Charlie, he was still asleep upstairs. Barry said he had seemed very fatigued lately. Restaurant work wasn't easy, and it was even harder in six-inch heels.

"What's done is done," I said, and Barry agreed. "Luke's ready with breakfast. Try to take it easy today, okay?" We hung up.

"All good?" asked Luke as he arranged the plates on the table.

"So far."

"Let's hope it stays that way. Listen, I think I need to go check on my father today. I'm gonna head on over there after we eat and shower."

"Sounds like a plan," I said, and reached for the coffee cup. "I need to swing by Mom and Dad's anyway. I could use the distraction."

We ate with very few words said between us. I was never known as the silent type, but there were times that I could appreciate these moments. This was one of them. Luke finished reading the sports section while I looked at the society pages. The debutante balls and coming out parties had begun. These were not my people and we would never have run in the same circles, but now that Lana was on board at the Duke, I started recognizing more of them as our clients. Things were running fairly smoothly between us. No blowups yet. It was a pleasant surprise. When breakfast was over, we cleared the dishes, got ready and went our separate ways.

"Say hello to Red and Rosa for me," I said as we walked to our cars.

"Will do. Give your parents a hug."

I started Lady up and backed out of the drive, but instead of turning left towards Mom and Dad's place, I headed out in the opposite direction. Something was pulling me towards the lake, and I wasn't sure why. Maybe I just needed to reflect on the past few weeks. Driving these back roads put me at ease, and it calmed me to see the changes that had taken place in Parkville. There were new subdivisions where old farms used to be, country roads that suddenly connected through to new highways, and old homesteads that had simply aged gracefully as the world matured around them. I was lost in thought when my phone started buzzing. It was Barry, so I pulled over into the old church parking lot where I had learned to drive, and I put Lady in park.

"Hey, I'm just out driving," I started.

"Derek, I need your help!" He was crying, sobbing, his words tumbling over each other in between gasps for air. "I'm at the hospital. I called 911. I had to call an ambulance. I need you to meet me here as soon as you can."

"*What's happening?* Are you okay? Are you hurt?" He had me nervous as hell and my heart started pounding furiously.

"It's Chinois. *Charlie.* I found him on the bathroom floor upstairs. He was passed out. Unconscious. I don't know how long he'd been like that. The lady on the line talked me through it as best as she could. They have him in a room now and they won't let me see him. I'm at the hospital. The waiting room. I'm scared." He could barely keep it together.

"Okay, okay, I need you to breathe, alright? I'm on my way. Just hang in there. I'm coming."

■■■

It is a cliché to hate the smell of hospitals, but some clichés are so grounded in truth that you cannot avoid them. As I entered through the sliding emergency room doors I was hit by the clinical scent of chemicals and death. It frightened me, but I knew I had to be calm for Barry. He needed me. I saw him immediately in the waiting area, seated on a brown pleather chair against a cold, grey wall with a bright yellow painted graphic that said 'Welcome!' above his head. As if anyone would choose to be in a hospital. He was so pale, his eyes staring off into the distance for answers.

"Barry!" I called out.

He looked over to me, leapt to his feet, and then threw himself in my arms.

"I didn't know what to do. I didn't know what to do," he cried.

"It's okay, it's okay. You did the right thing." I held him tight and rocked him slowly until the sobbing subsided. I sat him down next to me, then reached for the tissue box so he could blow his nose. It was so light that I knew it was almost empty. Why was I even thinking about that? I had to stay focused. "Tell me what happened."

He wiped his tears and collected himself. I could practically see his heart pounding through his shirt. He looked desperately sad, his lips trembling at the corners. "After we hung up, I finished my breakfast. Charlie usually sleeps a bit later than me. He's always so tired. I figured it was just the stress of working on his feet all day at the restaurant. I've been noticing though that he seems to get out of breath when he climbs the stairs to his bedroom. He's up in my old room. But I just ignored that. I mean, we're getting older, right? It's normal. I was about to go run some errands when I realized I hadn't heard a peep from him. Nothing since yesterday when he left for his afternoon shift and I went to the Bears' Club for the fundraiser. I called upstairs to check on him this morning and he didn't answer. Something didn't feel right, so I went up. That's when I found him collapsed on the bathroom floor in his underwear. Oh, Derek, *he's so thin.* I mean, I knew he was small. As Chinois he's larger than life, but as Charlie, he's just so thin. And I saw a lesion. He has a lesion on his back. I didn't... I didn't know it was so bad. I had no idea."

I pulled him in and held him tighter. Was that why Charlie had left New York without so much as a glance over his shoulder? It all started to make more sense now.

"Mr. Henry?" A nurse called out from the reception desk.

"Yes, that's me." Barry looked up.

"If you'll just walk through the door Dr. Goldman will see you now."

"Thank you."

We got up, threw away our wet tissues, then walked into the unknown.

■■■

"You did everything you should have done," the doctor told us as we stood in the hallway. "His vitals are stabilized. We have him on fluids. We're doing everything we can to make him comfortable."

"Is he dying?" asked Barry softly.

"No need to worry about that today. We've rebalanced some of his medications so I think we can get him back on track. He told me he has been working more on his feet, and I think that just caught up with him. He needs rest. We have him on oxygen, but he should be able to talk to you, if you'd like that. You're welcome to see him."

"Yes, I'd like that very much. Thank you, Dr. Goldman."

You are never fully prepared to see a friend or loved one hooked up to machines. He was propped up in the bed, his eyes closed, but they popped open as we approached his bedside.

"I wish you'd told me you were coming," he said. "I'd have worn something nicer. I never looked good in an assless gown."

"Nobody does, my dear," said Barry, shaking his head. "Nobody does."

"You scared us," I said. "But the doctor says you're going to get better. You just need some rest."

"No rest for the wicked," he said, then started coughing. "I don't plan to rest. No time for that. I still have things I want to do. I haven't asked George Clooney to marry me yet."

"I think he's taken now," said Barry. "We'll find you somebody else."

"Well, he hasn't met *me* yet. Apparently, I make quite an impression."

"That you do. But let's concentrate on getting you better first. We don't want George to see you like this. Especially under these fluorescent lights."

"Oh, I know. The worst. When I get out of here, let's say you and I invest in a hospital just for gays, with no overhead lighting and some nicer gowns. We can base them on vintage Halston."

"You can count on that my friend."

As I stepped out to let them have their moment alone, I couldn't help but to think of my own friends who would be there for me if I ever needed them. And no, they would never allow overhead lighting either.

■■■

Charlie spent three days in the hospital before they discharged him. The doctor said that he should be back to his normal self eventually, but that he needed to rest for at least a week first. Barry and Tucker set him up in the bedroom downstairs, and Barry moved his own things back up to his former room.

It had been a very trying week for all of us, so we were really looking forward to something fun. Tommy's birthday was this weekend and he had requested a full night at Chesty Cheese, complete with cocktails, gourmet pizzas, and a few trips to the champagne room. Peaches had set us up with the best table in the house, right in front of the main stripper pole. The whole Scooby Gang was in attendance: me and Luke, Tommy and Meredith, Kit and Shawn, and a very pregnant Bammy and Michael.

"You sure you can fit that stomach under the table?" I teased her.

"I am *not* that big yet. Just you wait. I can do better."

"*You. Look. Great!*" said Kit. "I'm just happy you could come out. That'll all change when you have the baby. We'll never see you again." She frowned.

"Oh, that's just not gonna happen," said Bammy. "Michael and I have already agreed. It's so much cheaper to have a babysitter than to get a divorce."

"Red and Rosa have already volunteered," said Michael.

"Don't get any ideas about signing us up for that," I said to Luke.

He narrowed his eyes. "You act all mean, but you're aware we all know that's an act, right?

"Stop, Luke. You'll confuse him," said Kit. "He likes to think we haven't figured him out."

"Anyone mind if we move on from the Derek Show?" said Tommy, raising his hand. "It's my birthday!"

"Yes, the man is right," I said and clapped my hands together. I was eager to save discussions of my psyche for a future therapy session. "What would you like to drink, birthday boy?"

"The blood of my enemies!"

"Eight cosmopolitans, coming right up." Everyone laughed.

"Make mine a virgin," reminded Bammy.

"That's what she said," said Tommy, as if that joke had never gotten old.

■■■

The birthday boy was back in the champagne room enjoying the first of what would be many private lap dances that night. Peaches kept the drinks flowing, and Kit took advantage of her front row seat more than anyone else.

"I like to hand out the singles," she said. "I feel like a dirty Santa Claus."

Everyone was getting very toasted and I was happy that there were no designated drivers tonight. Tucker had arranged a limo to take all of us home at the end of the evening, so everyone was imbibing to the max.

"I like people," I overheard a slurring Meredith say. "I hate woodchucks."

Aisha stopped by our table to snap a few pictures. She was everywhere these days: weddings, parties, events. I'm glad she had found a more creative job than door girl at the Bongo Room. Shawn stood up to give her a hug.

"Hey, y'all know how I met Aisha?" he asked. "It's a funny story. I was waiting in line to get into the Bongo Room one night."

"This was before I started working there," she said.

"Exactly. Anyway, I was all alone and the line stretched down the block. This girl walked up to the front of the line, locked eyes with me and then came over and hugged me. I hugged back, of course. She said, 'Oh, my god! I'm so happy I found you. This line is crazy, right? Are you excited?' Then she leaned in and whispered in my ear, 'Be cool, please? I'll buy you a drink when we get inside.' And that was that!"

"Friends ever since," she said.

"Smooth!" said Kit. "I like a lady who knows what she wants. Speaking of, I need more singles, baby."

"How much have you spent?" he asked.

"I'm just having fun! And the ladies *love* me."

"I'm sure they do." He reached for his wallet, but Luke spoke up first.

"Let me get this," he said and turned to me. "Care to escort me to the ATM?"

"It would be my pleasure."

We walked past the stage lights and headed to the corridor to the left of the bar. He withdrew a few twenties then exchanged them for singles at the change machine. As we walked back up the hallway, he paused to push me against the wall and kiss me.

"I love that you get stripper money for my friends," I said between kisses. "That's true love."

"Good, because I can't return you. I'd never get my deposit back."

"Hey, I'm not *that* damaged."

"Not yet at least. I plan on doing plenty of damage in the years to come."

"You can count on that."

We kept making out against the wall. I opened my eyes while we kissed so I could see if he looked as handsome as I imagined, when I saw something just past his shoulder that made me quickly pull back.

"Wait. Stop," I said.

"Did I do something wrong?"

"No. Over there. In the back corner of the club. Do you see what I see, or am I drunker than I thought?"

He squinted his eyes and looked in the wrong direction.

"Not there. *There,*" I pointed, then quickly withdrew my hand.

I would have recognized that cream jumpsuit with the plunging neckline anywhere. What I wasn't prepared to see, however, were someone's hands all over her, with his mouth completely covering hers.

Well hello, Chip.

8

GLAMA GALS

Luke and I wisely decided to save the conversation with Lana for another day. We were both drunker than we needed to be, and besides, who were we to judge? Several times in the past we had reminded Lana to stay out of our bedroom, so didn't we owe her the same respect?

"I cannot *wait* to hear this story," I gasped.

"You'll *have* to wait," he said. "Right now, we need to get out of here. I don't want her to feel confronted or embarrassed. She'll tell us in her own time if she wants to."

"How can you be so level-headed after so many drinks?"

"Practice. I have to take care of you, don't I?"

We had one last smashing kiss before we headed over to our group to say we were calling it a night. Luke gave Kit and Shawn a stack of singles and we excused ourselves for the evening. Miraculously, Lana didn't notice us leave, or at least she pretended not to. That drama would be saved for another day. I couldn't help but to think of poor Sam and Crosby though. They would never forgive Chip!

The car dropped us off at home and then returned to wait for the others.

"I've been here before," I said, looking at the house.

"What was his name?" teased Luke.

"Cowboy. Coach. I don't know. Something hot. All I remember is that his doorbell didn't work."

■■■

All of Parkville came out to pay their last respects to Mayor Edward 'Belle' Bellman. The church pews were packed, with standing room only at the back. Speaker after speaker spoke effusively of Edward Bellman's many accomplishments and legacies. Not a soul mentioned Belle. I felt like I was at one funeral today, but wished I had been able to attend two. It didn't feel right.

"He passed peacefully in the bed at my side," Bitsy

Bellman told one friend, recounting how she found him in the morning. The mournful widow looked elegant as she greeted each and every attendee after the services, the lie building with each retelling. How she managed to move him from the toilet seat we would never know.

There was a whisper in the crowd at the reception that a hint of lipstick had been found on his neck and it wasn't Bitsy's shade. The gossip traveled through the room while the crowd ate finger sandwiches and drank sweetened iced tea.

"Come on back to the house, will you?" asked Red. "I'm gathering a few of Belle's friends to reminisce. We need to be able to speak freely in order to properly mourn."

"Of course," nodded Luke.

We followed the row of cars out from the parking lot and made our way to the Walcott house. Rosa greeted us at the door with a warm hug. She had prepared light snacks, but Red waved them off. His friend had passed on and all he wanted was bourbon. He led us back to his study, the enormous windows flooding the room with light. He pulled the drapes to block out the outside world, poured himself a healthy drink, and sat silently in his leather chair. The doorbell rang and Barry and Lloyd Barton were soon ushered in. Rosa knew better than to ask if we needed anything else. Red's face was stoic. She shut the heavy door as the silence filled the room, each man lost in contemplation as they stared at their quickly depleted glasses. I glanced at Luke, unsure of what to do or say, so I did what I did best; I refilled all of their drinks and sat back and waited. I had a feeling that my patience would pay off. Finally, after two refills, Lloyd broke the malaise.

"What *are* we doing here, Red? The man is dead. There's nothing left to say."

Red broke his longstanding gaze with his bourbon and looked up to face Lloyd. "Oh, I believe there is. There's been too much unsaid for too many years. It's time we spoke it out loud."

Barry looked visibly nervous as he shifted in his seat.

What was going on here?

"I disagree," said Lloyd. "We agreed years ago to keep the past buried. That agreement has served us well all this time. Why should that change now?"

Red stared at him, unblinking. "We took an oath as Glama Gals to support one another. We broke that oath, and everything went wrong. That decision has plagued me for years. I will not go to my grave with that on my conscience, as Belle did. I intend to meet my creator with a clear heart, devoid of guilt. We ran that boy off, Lloyd, and it wasn't right, damn it. *It wasn't right!"*

His voice raged and my eyes widened, startled. I shot Luke a look of furrowed brows.

What boy is he talking about?

If I had learned anything since I came back home it was to keep my mouth shut as the stories unfolded in front of me. I didn't need to add anything, there was already enough tension in the room. The drinks were emboldening them to speak. Barry hadn't said a word though. He looked as if he wanted to flee, but felt chained to the chair.

"This was not my doing," said Lloyd. "This was all Edward. He should never have led that boy on. Any fool could see that Stevie was in love with him. The way that boy followed him around like a puppy dog was despicable. People talked. The Glama Gals were just for a lark. A laugh. We never hurt anyone."

"But we did," said Barry quietly. "We did."

The room turned to face him, a mixture of fear, anger, resentment, and sadness on their faces. Luke and I just looked bewildered.

Why were they letting us hear all of this?

"When Red and I started the Glama Gals, it was for fun, yes. You joined us Lloyd, then Edward and Stevie." Barry glanced at me, as if to explain. "Remember, at that time, drag was a laugh. It was comedy. We were just college kids having a joke. We were a hit at parties, and no one thought anything of it. We all had girlfriends, so there was no question that we were straight. Red was dating Posy, I was dating Janey, Edward was with Bitsy. Only Lloyd and Stevie were single. Lloyd, you were chasing every girl in town. But Stevie. Poor Stevie. He only had eyes for Edward. And that just wouldn't do. It wasn't safe."

"It was just plain stupid," said Lloyd. "Stevie went too far. He should have known better."

"Known better than to have fallen in love?" said Red, his voice once again filling with anger. "How dare you, in the presence of my son. Who are we to say that one love is right, and another is wrong? I loved Posy. Edward loved Bitsy. Even Barry loved Janey in his own way."

"But Edward did not love Stevie!" said Lloyd as he slammed his drink on the table. "That was unreciprocated. I don't care how much you say he led him on. Admiration is one thing, but Stevie crossed a line when he expected more. When he *wanted* more. He should have never kissed Edward at that party. Edward was not the right person for Stevie. Edward had every right to deck him, and everyone knew it! We all felt the same, you cannot deny it."

"I didn't," said Barry.

"Neither did I," said Red.

"I was just too afraid to speak up," said Barry. "I was dealing with my own demons. My own fears of being caught. Janey, too. She had her 'friendship' with Mabel. I had my trips to New York. Together, we had each other, and we knew exactly why. We had no idea that the world would evolve as it did. If we had known back then what we know today, I would have done so many things differently."

"We ostracized that poor boy," said Red. "Made him feel unworthy. What we did was unforgivable, and I do not blame him for fleeing. But we robbed him of his youth, of his love for love. We robbed him of his family, and they him. They never got to see what became of him. We erased him from our world as if he never was a part of our lives, as if he had never existed. No one talks about Stevie. We are all ashamed. I can only hope and pray that he found a life more worthy of his love, of the light that shone so brightly through him. I hope he is happy. I hope he has a family and friends who support him and care for him, as we were unable to do because of our own faults, our own misgivings, our terrible, inadequate insecurities. Imagine what he would say to us today, seeing us gather for Edward's burial. Would he be kind? Would he be cruel, as we were to him? Or would he be grateful, gracious to be included? What would he say to Derek, especially? After all these years?"

I looked up, shocked to suddenly hear my name.

"Excuse me?" I said timidly. "I don't even know who Stevie is or was. Why would he care about what I think?"

"Because, Nephew," said Barry solemnly. "Stevie's your uncle. Johnny's older brother."

■■■

Everything stopped. Luke reached for my hand, but I didn't know what to do. I was sure my mouth was wide open. The world went quiet and I felt numb.

"Derek? Derek, are you okay?" Luke shook me out of my reverie.

I could taste metal in my mouth, so I took a big swig of bourbon and swallowed hard

"I have another uncle?" My mind was racing. "How? How is that possible? What kind of monsters are you? Is he dead? Alive? Do any of you care?"

"I'm so sorry," said Barry, tears forming in his eyes. "I know it sounds awful, but after he left town, he just disappeared. Everywhere. In our words, in our thoughts. From your dad's family. They knew about him, of course. There were rumors. They suspected that he was gay, though it was never said out loud. Your dad's parents were farmers, remember? They didn't understand Stevie. They couldn't. It was a different time. The years passed and no one heard from him and they just let it be. Johnny married Audrey, you were born, then your dad took off on his own and disappeared for many years, as well. The town just accepted that that was what the Walters did. They left. When you announced that you were going to New York at least we were grateful that we knew your destination. We didn't expect you to come back either, but you did."

"Please, you cannot blame Barry," Red said, speaking up. "He did what we all did. He got in line. It was what we were told to do. It is easy now to say that Edward overreacted by lashing out at Stevie, but as Barry said, the times were different. In his mind he was defending his honor. We did not have the choices then that you have today. I am sorry. I truly am. After Stevie disappeared, our lives changed. The Glama Gals were no more. Edward changed. He focused on Bitsy. It was only years later when we founded the Bears' Club that we rediscovered our passion for vaudeville, burlesque, and comedy. Edward brought Belle out of hiding, and I think that rekindled his joy for life. Seeing you with Luke when you first started dating, however, just brought all of that fear back to me. You were Stevie in that scenario, and Luke was Edward. I was afraid for you, afraid for my son. It took so much for me to move on from the thoughts that were holding me back. Watching the struggles that you two encountered and the final acceptance you achieved in this town gave me hope that Stevie found that, wherever he may be. But knowing that we kept his memory subdued has haunted me all of these years. When Belle passed, I knew that I had to correct that. I can only hope you will forgive us, forgive me."

I wasn't sure what I was feeling. My head was in a whirlwind. I needed to talk to my dad. I just felt like running.

See, I am a Walter.

"I, on the other hand, do not seek forgiveness," said Lloyd. "We did what we had to. We all made choices and we have to live with those. I see no benefits in rehashing this."

"You're such an entitled prick." I spat the words at him.

"You should be more careful," he said. "I own half this town."

"*And I own the other half,*" said Red standing. "I think you may have overstayed your welcome, Lloyd. I thank you for taking the time to hear me out today. I am certain it was the right thing to do. Now, however, I must ask you to show yourself out." He extended his hand towards the door. It was clearly a command and not an offer.

My legs were shaking, and Luke placed his arm around me to comfort me. I stared at Barry, unsure of what to say. Nothing, for now. I had to process.

"I need to get out of here," I said.

"Derek, I…" Barry said.

"No." I cut him off. "Luke, get me out of here."

■■■

He drove me straight to my parents' house without a single word uttered between us. He knew I needed to see my dad. His car had barely pulled in the drive when I opened the door and ran out towards the front door.

"Dad!" I yelled angrily as I burst through. "Johnny, where are you?"

My mom came out from the kitchen with a look of worried fear on her face. "What's wrong? Is something wrong?"

"I need to speak to Dad," I said, clearly upset. I looked to my right and I could see him through the window, seated on the porch. He stood to see what all the fuss was about.

"Audrey, why don't you and I take a walk," said Luke. "I can explain. But I think it's best we leave."

She looked at me with sad eyes and resigned herself to the situation. She removed her apron, tossed it onto the chair, and kissed me on the cheek as she passed through the room to the front door. Luke nodded to me, then left quietly.

"Call me when you need me," he said. And they were gone.

Dad had walked in from outside. He looked puzzled. "What's going on?" he asked.

"How could you do that?" I dove right in, spitting my words at him. "How could you do that to your own brother? Let him leave like that? How could you not tell me he even existed? What the *hell* were you thinking?"

Johnny paused, clearly affected by my words. He hit an imaginary wall and it stopped him in his tracks. He looked panicked, distraught. He regained his composure and walked slowly to the couch, reaching behind him to support himself as he sat.

"Stevie," he whispered. "Is he back?" He looked so sad that I realized immediately that I was attacking the wrong person. Dad didn't deserve my anger. He was just as hurt as I was. How could I have imagined otherwise?

I took a seat next to him and buried my face in my hands. "I'm sorry for yelling," I said, calmer. "I'm just freaking out. I need answers."

"It's okay," he said. "I probably deserved it. Tell me what happened."

I told him about the scene at Red's, about the story they recounted of Edward and Stevie. I told him how they all believed it was the right thing to do to just let him disappear, to erase him.

"I even called Lloyd a prick," I said.

"Well, I'm sure he's heard worse," he offered. He took a deep breath. "I'm not even sure where to start."

"Try the beginning."

"Stevie is my older brother," he started. "Growing up, he was our parents' favorite. He had a glow about him, a shine. He could light up a room instantly, like you can. I see him in you, sometimes. He was 'different,' though, when being different was not accepted as it is today. Even as kids we knew it. But he was my brother and I loved him. Until we got older and everything changed. I could sense everyone turning against him, and I followed their lead. I was a coward. I turned on my own brother. Ignored him, taunted him, teased him. I was the relentless little brother who suddenly found the power to be stronger than his older sibling. I never knew about Edward. Hearing that from you today actually makes me feel better, in a way. Now I understand why he left. For so many years I thought it was because of me, because of what I lacked, because of the way his own family treated him. I was ashamed. Years later, after your mother and I were married and you were born, well, that's when I cracked. Barry hated me. I never understood why, but I suspected it was partially because of Stevie and partially because I was not good at being a father. I wasn't ready for it. I could not commit myself to you and your mom one hundred percent and be the proper dad that I needed to be. When I left town, I could hear the cheers behind me. I imagined that was what Stevie felt. A sense of relief. It wasn't until years later that I realized that I had failed you all, failed myself. So, I came back. But Stevie never did. I was so used to not having him in my life, that I never knew how to bring his memory back, to you. I'm so sorry. I really am."

He fell into my arms and we hugged, the tears flowing freely. We had all been through too much to keep creating discord. We didn't need that.

"I just wish I could meet him, Dad."

"Me, too," he cried softly. "Me, too."

9

JOIN THE PARTY

I tried everything I could think of to find out any information on Stevie Ray Walter. He and Dad shared the same middle name, but beyond his brother's date of birth, Dad didn't have many more tangible details. My paternal grandparents had passed on, so there were very few other possibilities. Red's knowledge was outdated, Belle had passed on, and Lloyd wasn't an option, of course. Stevie must have changed his name; of that I was certain. Every possible clue fizzled out and led nowhere. I didn't want to give up, but I didn't have a choice.

"I don't even know where he went after Parkville."

Luke and I were discussing my efforts a few mornings later in bed. "It's like he just disappeared."

"He doesn't want to be found, I guess," he said. "It's not up to us to bring him back. He has to decide that on his own. Johnny returned because he needed to reconnect to you and your mom. You came back because you needed to find your purpose. Maybe he's happy where he is. Maybe the thought of this place carries too much sadness."

"But everything's different now," I said. "I'm here. Mom and Dad are married again. Barry is Beret. Hell, Chinois is working at Saul's and there's a line out front to get in. I want him to see all of that, to experience it. Parkville isn't what it used to be."

No matter how much I persevered, though, the fact remained. Stevie Ray Walter was lost to us and I couldn't bring him back. As Luke said, it would be up to him. I only hoped that the universe would send him a clue to find his way back home.

"I get that," said Luke. "But you can't keep chasing things that you can't change." He kissed me.

"I got you, didn't I? I'm a greyhound, remember?"

"Yes," he smiled. "Now go start breakfast, will you? I'm jumping in the shower. I'm meeting the team for an early run and if the coach is late, I'll never hear the end of it."

I shuffled towards the kitchen, started the electric kettle for the French press, and dropped two slices of sourdough into the toaster. The water began to bubble in the pot as I heard the familiar thwack on the front door and went to retrieve the newspaper.

"Holy shit," I said to myself as I read the headline. My phone buzzed and I didn't even have to look down to see who it was.

"Can you *believe* it?!" exclaimed Barry. "Is he delusional?"

"Yes, I believe he is."

...

There would be a special election in November to replace Edward 'Belle' Bellman as mayor of Parkville, and Lloyd Barton had announced his candidacy for the job. His platform was simple, intended to appeal to the kind of people he screwed over most often in life. Lloyd planned to run as a titan of business.

"It takes a businessman to understand what this city needs," he expressed in the article. "Edward Bellman was a fine man, and he tried his best, of that I have no doubt. I honor his memory. But there are things I can bring to the table that he could not. I've run many successful businesses in my life. When elected, I plan to surround myself with the best people, the smartest people. I will bring in those with knowledge of how to fix everything wrong with this town. Government is too big. Too many restrictions. They try to stop a man from succeeding. It's quite corrupt, they say. Well, I stand before you and tell you that I am incorruptible. Everyone knows I'm a millionaire already, so there's nothing that can sway me. I can't be bought. In fact, I won't even take a salary."

I folded the paper and flung it across the room in disgust. There was no way I would let Lloyd worm his way into that office.

Not gonna happen.

"Are you free for lunch today?" I asked my uncle. "Because we have work to do."

●●●

After a week of bedrest and an adjustment in her medication, Chinois was thankfully up and running again. She was only working lunch shifts for the moment so she could rest evenings. She had a brutally honest conversation with Saul and Rachel, and to their credit they were fully supportive of her desire to stay on at the restaurant. Rather than have her wait tables she assumed the role of hostess.

She enjoyed greeting customers and leading them to their tables, with a bit of extra snark along the way. Since most people were there to catch a glimpse of her anyway, this increased everyone's interactions with Parkville's latest obsession. Even though she was a feisty one, anyone could see she had really fallen for Parkville. Chinois now adorned her outfits with plastic sushi roll necklaces and had even replaced the paper lanterns in her enormous black wig with Saul's Sushi takeout boxes.

"Marge, you got some troublemakers coming your way," she teased as she led two men in business suits to their table. "This one pinched my ass. Watch out." The older of the two laughed out loud as his younger colleague blushed. "I've got my eyes you," she told him. "Well, the good one. But just in case you're faster than me and I lose sight of you, here's my number. Call me." She made her way up front and found me and Barry laughing with the rest of the crowd.

"You're a hit," I said, blowing an air kiss left and right.

"I haven't hit anyone!" she sneered. "You can't prove anything. Besides, there are no cameras here," she pointed around the room. "No evidence."

"Your very best table for two, please," said Barry.

"Two? Do you plan on leaving your backside *outside*? I think you may need a bigger chair."

"Look who's talking," he replied, looking her up and down. "It seems someone has been enjoying her fair share of pastrami pot stickers."

Chinois had been noticeably gaining weight since her hospitalization a few weeks ago, and we were all pleased to see her feeling better. She grabbed two menus and led us to a four top in the back.

"Blanche," she called out, "set these two up with a complementary chopped liver and soy cracker appetizer. It's to die for." She turned back to us with a stage whisper. "No, honestly, it'll kill you. Sent three men to the hospital last week and I just want to repay you the favor."

"She's not having a hard time fitting in," I said as she headed back up front.

"Definitely extra," said Barry, picking up Tucker's lingo.

We placed our order with Blanche and got straight to business.

"There has to be someone who can take on Lloyd," I said. "We can't let the people fall for his 'businessman' bullshit. How about Red? Do you think he'd do it?"

He shook his head. "Red's too private. The last thing he wants to do is expose his family to more public drama. Besides, he'd never divest himself of his holdings."

"Well you don't think Lloyd will, do you?"

"Hasn't he already?" he shrugged. "He sold you the Duke, Tucker has Gaycare. Rumor has it he's been selling off things left and right."

I sighed. He was right. "I had just hoped he was setting himself up for a nice retirement. He couldn't have known Belle would have a massive stroke and leave the door open for him to become mayor. I mean, I know he's a snake, but even this is beyond his power. There has to be someone."

We started to run through the list of all the men who attended Secret Sundays, then moved on the members of the Bears' Club. We knew which ones would immediately be Team Lloyd, so that knocked the majority off our list. There were a few wildcards, but no one clearly came to mind as a strong enough competitor.

"We need the anti-Lloyd," I said. "Someone who came from nothing, someone who has nothing to hide. Maybe even a small business owner, rather than another politician or millionaire. Someone who everybody loves."

"Hey, stable geniuses," said Chinois, towering over our table. "I couldn't help but overhear you. You're both about as subtle as a pair of drag queens in a wig shop. I may have just moved here, but I've already met most of the people in this burg. If you want the best candidate in town, you're ignoring the obvious."

"Who?" asked Barry.

"*That girl.*" Chinois pointed over our heads at the mirror on the wall behind us. We turned to see her finger directed squarely at Barry's head.

■■■

It took some convincing, but after a family discussion with Mom, Dad, and Tucker, Barry decided to go for it.

"Does that mean I'll be First Lady if you win?" asked Tucker.

"More like First Twink," said Barry.

"What can we do?" asked Dad. "How can we help?"

"We need a campaign manager," I said. "Someone who knows how to play to win and cut in line when the time is right. I have the perfect person in mind."

Aisha was more than happy to meet me and Barry at the Duke later that week. I asked Lana to join us as well. We had already successfully combined our forces at work, so it only made sense to include her in our political campaign.

"I've never done anything like this," said Aisha. "Are you sure you want me? I'm not exactly a Parkville insider. I don't run in the same circles as these guys."

"That's exactly *why* we want you," I said. "We can't

beat the businessmen at their own game. We have to play our own. We should accentuate our differences. Barry appeals to a different audience, and we have to play up his strengths. The youth vote will be everything, and between the Bongo Room and your photography business you have all the connections there."

"And I have access to all those rich, bored, housewives," said Lana. "Sure, some of them are sheep. They'll do whatever their husbands tell them to do. But you'd be surprised how many of them say one thing in public and then do another. No one's following them into that voting booth. We just have to convince them that Barry isn't a protest vote. He needs to come across as stable, an older pillar of this community."

"I'm not *that* old," he objected.

"My mind is already spinning," said Aisha, jumping in. "We can throw an epic event. Invite all the right people. Our social media game has to be on point. I have to ask, though. Are you planning on campaigning as Barry Henry or Beret?"

Barry took a deep breath, raised his eyebrows, and exhaled dramatically. "I hid Beret away for far too long. She's out now, that's for sure. But that's how I want to approach this. Honestly. Look, Belle was an open secret. Everyone knew, but no one spoke about her out loud in the press. I want to change that. No, I don't want to push Beret onto anyone who won't understand that side of me. But I won't hide her. If I'm asked, I'll be straightforward. So, to answer your question, Barry Henry is running for mayor of Parkville. *Proudly*."

"Then let's get to work," said Aisha, smiling. "We have a candidate to elect.

...

Aisha came back in a few days with a brilliant campaign concept. 'Barry Henry, a Mayor for Everyone.' The idea was to present Barry as a candidate who could cover all the bases and appeal to every socioeconomic class of Parkville. He had ties to the poor, middle and upper classes. He was friends with the older generation and the young. Straight, gay, or otherwise, everyone was his friend.

"He never met a cute guy he didn't like," offered Tucker.

"I think we'll skip that one," Aisha said wisely.

Lana and I organized a huge fundraising event at the Duke to launch Barry's campaign. So far, we hadn't encountered any public blowback. But something didn't feel right. Only time would tell if we would be successful. The night arrived and we were raring to go. The whole

Walter family, the Scooby Gang, and many others were helping to put the final touches in place before we opened the doors. Only a few prominent people were missing.

"Where's Red?" I asked.

Luke and Lana turned to each other, and then me.

"Father's staying neutral in this one, babe," Luke answered. "Of course, he's supporting Barry, but you know him. He stays above the fray."

I did know Red. And I knew what his words could do to help Barry get over the finish line. But this was one battle I would not win.

"All set, Crosby?" I asked. He was positioned behind the bar, as always.

"You bet," he answered. "Sam's ready to pass the welcome champagne and then he'll get the first round of hors d'oeuvres out. The bar is fully loaded."

"Well, let's make sure our guests get loaded, as well," said Aisha. "Happy people tend to open their pockets more easily. We need the help. Can I get a Team Barry cheer?"

"Team Barry!" we yelled.

The night went as smoothly as we could have hoped. Sam and Crosby kept the treats flowing, while Team Barry worked the room, taking checks, coins, promises, and even digital payments. Tucker had set us up with a fundraising app called 'Very Barry.' We could track donations, remind voters of the platform, and solicit help for fundraising calls. The candidate himself was working the room, and he was on fire! I was so proud of him. He came across as confident, happy, and secure in his ability to lead Parkville in the right direction.

"Hey, Boss!" said Crosby from behind the bar. "Mind if I take a little break? Can you run the show behind here for a bit while I go in the back and grab something?"

"I'll do it," said Luke. "I'm pretty handy with a cocktail. I live with Derek after all."

I took a look around the room at the crowd we had gathered. We had the youth vote for sure. There were the LGBTQs. We definitely had the middle class and the more liberal segment of the upper class. But where were our friends from Secret Sunday or the Bears' Club? Were they all really so loyal to Lloyd? What was I missing?

"Barry, something's going on here." I pulled him aside. "Take a look around the room. Where are the guys from your club?"

"I was afraid of this," he said. "Lloyd is not one to take a challenge lying down. He's done this before. Once when we had an election for officers at the Bears' Club, he put the screws to everyone to vote against the candidate that he had taken a disliking to, for whatever reason. He played dirty and started spreading gossip. I've witnessed it. Trust me, I was there."

"That's what you told me about that meteor that killed the dinosaurs," said Tucker.

Before Barry could volley back, Kit spoke up.

"That's it! A meteor! We need to find his kryptonite."

"But what could that be?" I asked. "He hasn't put on drag since college, and besides, we don't want to villainize that anyway. His businesses have all seemingly run above board. Do we need to get ahold of his taxes?"

"A friend of a friend of a friend of mine is a hooker," she offered. "Maybe we can get her involved? You know what they say, a politician can never be found in bed with a dead hooker."

"I don't think we should kill anybody just yet," offered Barry.

"We're not killing *anyone*," I said, holding my hands up. "We just need opposition research. We need something on him. There has to be something."

"I don't want to play this underhanded," said Barry, shaking his head. "If I'm going to win this, I want to win fair and square."

"I agree with you," said Aisha. "But that still doesn't mean we shouldn't do the research. Without calling anybody out, do we know any super conniving, sneaky people who will do anything to get their way, no matter the cost?"

"Excuse me," I said, imaginary lightbulbs popping over my head. "I think I may have an idea."

Lana and I were getting along like gangbusters, surprisingly, but that didn't stop me from recognizing her true nature. Lana, like Lloyd, could be a snake. More of a scorpion, actually. But this particular scorpion was now firmly on my team, and it was such an oversight for me to miss taking advantage of every one of her many skills. I walked over to the bar where Luke was still helping out.

"Have you seen your sister?" I asked. He shook his head 'no,' elbows deep in glassware and open bottles.

I glanced around the room and couldn't find her. I knew that she could come up with a way to get the other Bears' Club members to come out against Lloyd, or at least privately support Barry. I just needed to find her first. I bobbed through the crowd and made my way back towards the kitchen.

Maybe she's in the office? I thought, glancing up the stairs.

I saw the door to the library ajar to my right. We usually kept that room closed and only used it for smaller, private functions. I reached to pull the door shut when I saw movement in the back of the darkened room near the windows. I peeked through, and sure enough, there she was.

Making out with Crosby!

10

NO MORE SECRETS

"We need to talk later," I said to Luke as I returned to the bar.

"What's up?" he asked.

Before I could answer, Crosby tapped my shoulder and said, "Thanks, Boss. I'm back."

"You all refreshed?" I asked smiling.

He looked at me quizzically.

"Never mind," I said. I walked back over to Barry and Aisha. "Barry, I have an idea. But first we need to know what we're dealing with. Can you ask around at the club and see if Lloyd has said or done anything to sway the members?"

"I'm heading over there first thing in the morning for our monthly meeting. You'll know as soon as I do."

"Good. Because we can't go into this blind. The more we know the better."

■■■

The next day Barry called just after lunch and confirmed our worst suspicions. Lloyd had poisoned the well, but good. It seemed that he had called a special meeting and invited everyone but Barry. No one would tell him what had transpired, but the outcome was clear; they would vote for Lloyd over him, and they would not elaborate.

"If none of them will talk then we'll go to the source," I said. "How do you feel about paying Lloyd a visit?"

Lloyd Barton's family had made their money in the hotel and service industry. Whereas Red owned most of the commercial and residential property in Parkville, Lloyd owned the hotels and restaurants. It was a pretty even split. He had grown up on a sprawling estate by the river bend, just near the university campus. He and his wife had lived there for a short time together, but when their marriage fell apart Lloyd converted the grounds into Barton Springs

Spa and Hotel. His wife fled to parts unknown and Lloyd moved downtown just before the revitalization and gentrification process began. Downtown was not considered 'safe' back then, but he didn't care. The fewer visitors he had, the fewer prying eyes there were. He snapped up an old, out of business bank building for a song and turned it into a fabulous townhome for one. Fronted by two-story columns with an impressive dome and imposing stone steps leading to the doors, the residence came to be known as 'Barton Bank.' No one had ever pegged his sexuality as a definite this or that. Tucker would later enlighten us all by saying that Lloyd was probably pansexual. The fact that he and his wife never produced an heir was whispered to be a reason for their marriage falling apart, which led to continuing gossip about his private life. It was well known that he appreciated a variety of personal company, and there were even rumors that he had converted the original bank vault in the basement into a dungeon.

Barry placed the call and thankfully Lloyd accepted our invitation to meet. Aisha agreed that he would probably be more forthright with fewer witnesses, so we drove over alone for an impromptu meeting. We parked the car in the parking garage that only ever filled up on game day weekends and walked the block and a half to Barton Bank.

The air had turned crisp with autumn now in full swing, the trees dropping their orange and yellow leaves en masse to canvas the sidewalks. We climbed the stone steps and I admired the two large metal doors. The copper had ionized to a lovely green patina. There was no doorbell, but rather a large brass lion's head doorknocker with a ring through his gaping mouth. The knock echoed through the portal and we waited. I detected footsteps, a click, and then one enormous green door swung open.

"Well hello," said Lloyd. "Welcome." He held his hand out to usher us in and we stepped inside.

The rotunda had been converted to a main salon, with couches, end tables, and a large flower arrangement of stargazer lilies on a carved mahogany table. Looking up it felt cavernous, much larger than it seemed from the street. Off to each side were dark wood sliding doors, both closed off to us.

"I have two bedrooms," he said, as if to answer my wandering eyes. "One on either side. Everything on this floor is mirrored, one for one. The office in the back is now a kitchen and there is a small, internal courtyard, but it's a bit chilly out today so I thought we would carry out our business here, if that's alright."

"It's really stunning," I said admiringly. "Such a find."

"Yes, I do rather like to find buried treasure. I love

interior design, as you know. I'm a great fan of transformation. There is something about the challenge of envisioning a new world in an otherwise ordinary space that enthralls me."

"Is the vault intact?" I asked. "I'd love to see it."

His smile remained frozen; he was not amused. "Perhaps another time," he offered. "Vodka stinger?"

"Oh, yes please," said Barry. "Derek's driving."

"Water is fine, thank you," I answered.

He stepped behind what must have been an old teller window and prepared our drinks. Barry and I took our places on one of the couches in the center. Lloyd returned with a silver tray and set it on the coffee table as he took a seat on the opposing couch.

"Cheers," he said as we took a sip. "Now, doesn't that feel better with the pleasantries out of the way? Let's get to business, shall we? To what do I owe the pleasure of today's visit?"

I turned to look at Barry as his eyes danced my way. We hadn't planned this part. Clearly it was up to me.

"Congratulations on your mayoral campaign," I said, beginning as politely as I could. "It's clear you have a bit of a head start on us, but I think we can all agree that we would prefer a positive campaign to a negative one, no?"

He didn't react.

"The reason for our visit today is...exploratory." I searched for the words. "We had a fundraiser the other night for Barry, and it was quite clear that a certain segment of the population was missing, namely Secret Sunday and Bears' Club members. You wouldn't know anything about that, would you?"

Again, no reaction.

"Perhaps something was said to them? Inferred?"

Lloyd reached for his cocktail, took another sip, then simply stared at me blankly.

"Damn it, Lloyd!" Barry said, bursting. He had had enough. "What the hell did you do? You owe it to me to 'fess up. How in the hell is this fair?"

Lloyd slowly placed his cocktail back down on the table and calmly folded his hands in his lap. "Life is not fair, my friend. I simply spoke the truth. Or rather, explained what would happen if I *did* speak the truth."

"Are you serious?" asked Barry. "You'd do that? You'd break your oath."

"It's quite straightforward," he responded. "Elect me, and our private moments remain private. Sundays shall remain secret, and Bears can hibernate quietly in their clubs. No one shall find out what goes on behind closed doors. No one will even know who enters those doors. But vote for anyone other than me and I'll fling those private doors wide open. Secrets be damned."

Our eyes grew wider.

"I should be thanking you and Red for the idea, actually. You set it all up for me, after all. Need I remind you, I'm not the one who suggested that a body be moved. I'm not the one who initiated covering up a death. I'm not the one who has a darling, beloved, football hero son who could get caught up in such a twisted nightmare of police questioning. That would be just beyond the pale, wouldn't it?"

"You wouldn't dare," seethed Barry, aghast. "Red is our friend."

"Watch me," he enunciated slowly. "I have *nothing* to lose, while you all have *everything* to lose. What few secrets I have are notoriously undocumented. I'm just one man, with access to many. You, on the other hand, you would never do this to them. No, Barry, you are a much better man than me. I admit that. You're too kind. You don't play dirty. But me? Well, they just can't take that risk, can they?"

And that was that.

We stood up quickly and left without saying a word. I tried to slam the door dramatically but the damn pneumatic thingy at the top foiled my plan. We stood outside on the street staring at our feet.

"He's won," said Barry limply. "That's it. It's over."

"No, it's not. It can't be." I was angry.

"But it is. He's right. I can't risk you and Luke getting involved in that mess with Belle. We should never have agreed to Red's plan.

"We all got caught up it. It was the right thing to do, and I know Luke doesn't regret it at all. He did it for his dad. Red believes in honor and dignity and everything that it entails."

"Well, I don't see a way out of this." He looked dejected.

"We can't give up yet. I won't allow it. I won't allow Lloyd to control all the strings. There has to be something."

But to be honest, I didn't see it. Yet.

■■■

I had no choice but to be an open book with Aisha.

"I honestly did not think that there was anything left in this town to shock me," she said admiringly. "Damn. Y'all are definitely crazy."

"I know." I buried my head in my hands. "But there must be something. There has to be. We're down to our last card to play. I just hope Lana can deliver."

Aisha and I headed over to the country club where Lana had booked her usual table. I was surprised, however, to see that Amber was seated with her.

"Derek! Over here!" Amber's hand shot up and waved about, her many gold bracelets jangling down her arm. She had money; of that we were all aware. But the new money would never alter who she was at the core.

"Wow," I said, "what a surprise to see you here." I glanced at Lana quizzically while Amber reached up to hug my neck.

"Amber's here to help us out," explained Lana. "You need devious, right? Well I can't think of two more devious women than us."

I narrowed my eyes. "I feel trapped. If I agree, I'm in trouble. If I disagree, I'm lying."

"Exactly!" said Amber. "Gotcha!" She sipped her vodka and diet soda through her straw and smiled.

"Now how can we help?" asked Lana.

I introduced Aisha to Amber and then filled them in on the few details that I could. I only said that Lloyd was holding something over Red and Luke, and if the news was released, it wouldn't be good for anyone. It wasn't up to us to fix that issue specifically, though. What we needed to do was find a way to make Lloyd back down, without spilling everything he knew.

"Barry wants to play fair," I said. "Our goal isn't to expose anyone. We may just want to *remind* Lloyd of a few things that he'd rather not let see the light of day. We just have to figure out what those things are."

"He's threatening *my family*," said Lana seething. "That's all I need to know. We're in."

"What have you got so far?" asked Amber.

"Not so much," I answered dejectedly. "He's a very, very private man. He's an only child, as far as I know. His family ran restaurants and hotels."

"Barton Springs Spa," said Lana.

"Amongst others," I nodded. "He's owned various restaurants about town, including the Duke. His businesses seem to be on the up and up. He's been divesting things, though, at a rapid rate lately, and we're not sure why."

"And the club memberships are off limits, right?" she asked, hinting at Secret Sunday and the Bears' Club.

"Correct. We don't want to expose anyone to friendly fire."

"Can we get to his finances? See if he pays his taxes properly?"

"We thought of that," I said, nodding at Aisha. "But that's probably not a possibility either. We can research everything that is publicly available, but he's a smart man. I doubt he'd make an accounting mistake. When he sold me the Duke all the paperwork was perfect."

"This is easy," said Amber with a great big smile on her face. "Y'all are making this easy for me, right? So I'll feel included?"

We all looked at her, puzzled.

"You're not?" she said and cocked her head sideways. "But it's so obvious."

"Spit it out, Amber," pushed Lana.

"*It's the wife*. The wife knows everything. Trust me, I know. I've been married five times." She stopped and counted on her fingers. "Wait, six. Yeah, six. I always forget that short one. The marriage wasn't short, the guy was, and he just seems to slip my mind kinda easy."

"We don't know anything about his wife," I said. "The marriage was short-lived, they had no kids, and she doesn't live here anymore."

"Exactly," said Lana. "I heard she went crazy. They say she's in some mental institution somewhere."

"I heard that she got tired of his cheating and ran away to live in the Caribbean," I said. "No one ever talks about her."

"Because he doesn't want you to," said Amber.

Was she smarter than all of us?

"What are you saying?" I asked.

"Listen, some people love weddings. Some people love

marriage. Me, I love husbands. Until I get tired of them of course, and then I look for the next one. There's just a limited number of eligible men in this town and I've made it my purpose to know as much about them as I can. No matter the age. I'll tell you everything I know about Lloyd Barton. All you have to do is ask."

"Go on," I prompted.

"To start with, he was a confirmed bachelor for years. Now, you're probably thinking what I am, but I could never get anyone to say it out loud. No one would tell me he was actually gay, but there were rumors. He was only married once, and it was much later than all of his friends. You're right that not much is known about her. But I did find out that he is *still* married. They never divorced. Once I discovered that I stopped poking my nose around. I mean, why bother when he's taken already? Are we getting another round?" She looked around for the waiter.

"Amber, I'll buy you a whole damn bar if you can find out more," I said eagerly. "Do you think you could dig around? How do you find this stuff?"

"Oh, I have my secrets."

It seemed everybody did.

■■■

Now that we had decided to focus on the wife, we all went our separate ways with specific goals. We decided to set up a meeting at the Duke when we had something good. I went straight to Barry to ask him questions about Lloyd's marriage.

He shook his head. "I don't believe I ever met her. By the time she entered the picture, we had all gone our separate ways. Red and Lloyd traveled in their circles, while Janey and I traveled in ours. They really didn't overlap. We had been friends, sure, but with marriages and kids, we all grew apart. Edward and Bitsy didn't socialize with any of us. There was really a sour taste in our mouths after the whole Stevie episode. I'm just sorry I can't help you more. I know you're doing all this for me."

I called Red and spoke to him, but he wasn't able to offer much more in the way of useful information, either.

"I remember she was European," he said. "She had an accent. Posy and I only met her a handful of times at social gatherings. Your uncle is right. After the Glama Gals disbanded, I really did not see Lloyd as much. And then we basically became business rivals, so that kept us separated as well. I do know that their marriage was very short-lived. She left rather quickly. I believe she went back to Europe. That is all I am able to remember."

Mom couldn't offer any help, either. She was a single

mother at the time. She and Dad had already divorced, and he was living on the west coast. Besides, she was never friends with that group.

We accomplished very little in the way of digging up new information and Barry was resigned to lose the campaign. Aisha tried to lift his spirits as the polls showed the numbers to be incredibly competitive, but he felt that without the business community's support he was destined to fail.

Lana and I were commiserating in our office at the Duke. She hadn't been able to come up with anything, either. She had checked the library to try and find information about Lloyd's wedding in the society pages, but unfortunately the microfiche from that decade had been damaged years ago when they updated to a digital filing system. We needed a lucky break, a *deus ex machina*.

Lana's phone buzzed. It was Amber.

"Hey, don't move! I'm on my way to meet you. I've got something."

The next fifteen minutes felt like an hour.

"How could she have found something we didn't?" I wondered.

Lana shook her head. "She's pretty nosy."

We heard the footsteps coming up the stairs and Amber entered our office with a plastic grocery store bag in her hand.

"I'm not nosy," she corrected Lana, "I just know who to ask. And I have great hearing." She reached into the bag and pulled out a dusty old photo album, the kind with the plastic-covered sticky pages. She flipped halfway through, then slammed her finger down on an old newspaper clipping that had weathered to a brittle yellow over time. The black and white image was muddled, but the caption was clear as day. "There she is. *Sunny Nyquist Barton*."

11

STAND AND DELIVER

Sure enough, there was a young Lloyd Barton standing next to his bride, Sunny Nyquist, cutting their wedding cake in a small private ceremony at his parents' estate by the river bend. We were dumbstruck. Amber had really come through for us.

"Where did you find this?!" I asked.

"Miss Addie. She just loves scrapbooking. Every time Jett won some football game or a cross-country race, she clipped the articles out of the paper and put them in a binder for him. Honestly, she's just better at that than I am. I was sitting at the kitchen table trying to come up with a way to find Lloyd's wife when Addie walked in and asked if there was anything else that I needed before she left for the day. I figured why not ask her. Turns out she's a big fan of weddings, too. She's been clipping and saving the announcements for years. I followed her home and we spent a good amount of time flipping through her books, and then this just popped out at me. There she was!"

"Amber, you're the best. This is amazing! Now we have a name."

"Nyquist," said Lana. "I don't remember any Nyquists in town."

"Red said she was European, with an accent," I reminded her. "She must be Swedish or Danish or something. It can't be that hard to find a Sunny Nyquist, right?"

We got online and started sleuthing through the internet. We couldn't find any Sunny Nyquist listed anywhere, but there were plenty of references to S. Nyquist in both Sweden and Denmark. Hundreds, actually.

"This'll be impossible," I said.

"Don't be such a loser," Lana harrumphed. "I don't partner with people who give up so easily."

"Well what are we supposed to do?" I asked.

"Start compiling email addresses, phone numbers, whatever you can find. I'll write something up and we'll start sending everything off. It's a needle in a haystack for sure, but we don't have any other choice. I am not letting that jerk threaten our family. Are you with me or not?"

"I am." She said *our* family.

Damn it, Lana, stop making me like you more.

It took us several hours to send everything out, but she was right. Reaching out to hundreds of strangers was our only hope. We copy pasted, printed letters, and fired of every possible request for information that we could. All that was left to do now was wait.

■■■

A few weeks passed and we found ourselves in the midst of a crisp October. I realized that I had been so busy with work that I hadn't gone to one football game this season. Luke had coached the Parkville High Commodores through a major winning streak, and I wanted to show my support for the last big match up before the playoffs.

"I'm coming to your game tonight with Bammy, Kit, and Tommy," I told Luke over lunch at the Tater Tot.

"You can't do that," he said, putting his beer down on the table.

"What do you mean I can't do that?"

"You just can't," he said matter-of-factly. "We've been winning."

"Yeah, and I'm sorry I haven't been there to see the games. I've been crazy busy."

"I know. And we've been winning. So, *you can't come.*"

I was flustered. "Wait, is this a superstitious thing?"

He took another long sip from his draft beer and smiled. "Look, I've got my game day underwear on. I'm not jinxing this. You know I love you, but I can't have you there, okay?"

"Oh, my god," I laughed. "You're something else. Bammy's gonna be pissed at me. She's almost seven months pregnant and she begged us to take her to the game tonight."

Luke sighed. "Well, you're gonna have to listen from the parking lot. I can't have you in the stands."

"So, you mean I can avoid sitting my ass on those hard, splintered bleachers, stay away from the crushing crowds of crazy parents, and have my own tailgate party with my friends at the car?"

"Yes. Please?" he begged.

"It's a deal."

We finished our lunch and headed home. Luke wanted to study his game plays, so I took the opportunity to go through some emails on the back terrace. So far there were no positive responses from any of the S. Nyquists that we had reached out to. The few responses we did receive were polite dead ends.

My phone hummed and it was Dad calling.

"I think I found him. I think I found Stevie."

I sat up quickly in my chair. "How? What happened?"

"I felt really awful after our conversation. I've just been haunted by the memories. I couldn't let you down, so I started looking for him. I remembered that my brother went down to Mardi Gras in New Orleans once. I'd never seen him happier than he was when he returned from that trip. I figured he must have run away to a place that made him happy. I started digging and I couldn't find any Stevie Walter in Louisiana, but I did find a Steven Ray. The phone number is unlisted, but I have an address. It's a long shot, but I'm driving down there tonight. I'll give you updates from the road."

"Good luck, Dad. Drive safely. I love you."

As a Southerner, I loved a good tailgate party. As a man who hated crowds, I loved a tailgate party where I could skip the game even more.

"This isn't as bad as I thought," said Bammy. We had

set up a lounge chair for her in the back of Tommy's pickup truck. An upside-down crate next to her chair was the perfect side table for her snacks and refreshments, and she was all snuggled up in a heavy quilt from home. Tommy's radio was tuned to the game and we had a Bluetooth speaker blaring the play by play.

"I feel like I'm in the olden days," said Kit. "It's kinda fun imagining the game in my mind."

"I know it's crazy," I said. "But Luke insisted."

"Shawn does the same stuff. He had this lucky guitar pick that he bought online. Supposedly it was signed by Kurt Cobain. His name was scrawled on it with a Sharpie. One night after a gig he couldn't find it and freaked out. I calmed him down and told him we'd look for it the next day. I woke up early, pulled another dirty pick from his stash and signed it with Kurt's name, myself. He had so many pictures of the thing that it was easy for me to copy. He was thrilled and none the wiser."

"You're awful," said Bammy. "I love it!"

"Don't any of you *dare* tell him. He still carries that thing around like it's sacred."

"Meredith has a lucky hat," said Tommy. "The one she wore when we met."

"*That's. So. Sweet,*" said Kit. She warmed her hands with her spiked cocoa.

"Michael has sex socks," said Bammy, raising one eyebrow and smirking.

"What the *hell*?" I laughed.

"He'd kill me if I told any of you this. It's ridiculous. He wore them on the night I'm pretty sure I conceived, so now he thinks they're magical. He's keeping them in a special place in his drawer so we can pull them out one day for baby number two. He refuses to let me wash them."

"Men are so damn weird," I said. "Here's to all these superstitions helping us to win the game today. Cheers!"

We continued to drink, tell stories, and catch up. Tommy was upgrading a few of the rooms at the Walcott's place. Rosa wanted everything ready when the baby arrived, just in case Michael and Bammy decided to spend the night there occasionally. She was very excited about being a grandma. It meant a lot to Red. My dad had a new show opening up at Kit and Meredith's gallery in November. He had been working with sculpting the human form out of natural found materials like driftwood and stones. It was a new format for him, a real departure from his metal sculptures, and they were very excited to see how they would be received. Dad's art was a real money maker and I was very proud of him.

"Two minutes left in the game," said Tommy, bringing us back into focus. We were up so many points that there was no way the other team could catch up. Now we were just running out the clock. With one final play to go, the opposing team had possession of the ball. A mad scramble ensued, but nothing came of it, and Parkville won the game!

"Guess who's getting lucky tonight!" I sang.

■■■

I let Luke sleep in the next morning as I got up and retrieved the morning paper. Lloyd was still ahead in all the polls, but just slightly within the margin of error. There was still hope for us after all. Barry had a huge number of followers interacting in the Very Barry app, sharing stories and supportive messages. I checked my emails and there were no responses from Scandinavia that helped us in the search for Sunny Nyquist. Dad had sent me a text message that he had arrived safely in New Orleans after having driven most of the night. He was planning on seeing if this Steven Ray was his brother. What if it was him, but he just hadn't wanted to be found and he reacted poorly when Dad showed up? The thought of that made me so nervous for him.

"Did you see the paper?" asked Barry. Our morning phone calls had become a habit of sorts. "Neck and neck, but he's still slightly ahead."

"It pisses me off," I said. "He's twisting the arms of these men and scaring them into voting for him."

"Manipulation through fear. That's not a new concept. Any news on Sunny?"

"Nothing yet. I've had a few people respond to the mails we sent out, but they've all been dead ends."

"I went to see Red. I asked him to speak to Lloyd to see if he could talk some sense into him. Lloyd's always been a bit of a loner, but I know he respects Red as a rival. Red tried, but it went about as well as you could imagine. Lloyd's sticking to his guns. He really doesn't care about anyone but himself. Red even offered to sell him some property that he has always coveted. No deal."

"Red did that for us? That was kind of him."

"He's a good man. He just wants the best for everybody. I don't know. Maybe I should just go ahead and drop out. Better to do that than be labeled a loser, right?"

"Don't you dare! We're not done yet. Get on your Very Barry app and let your fans hype you up some more."

"I told Tucker that if I won, we could take a long weekend trip to New York to celebrate. He asked if we could have breakfast at Tiffany's."

"He did *not*."

"He did. I didn't have the heart to tell him. At least if I lose then I can save him from finding out it's just a jewelry store."

Soon after we hung up Dad sent me a text message. Unfortunately, it was not the news we wanted. The Steven Ray he found in New Orleans was not his brother, but the gentleman thanked him for the visit, nonetheless. As a consolation they walked over together to Café du Monde and had beignets and coffee. He said goodbye to his new friend and started on the long drive back home.

■■■

We had a scheduled staff meeting on Monday morning at the Duke. Lana and I regularly met with Sam, Crosby, and our chef to plan the upcoming parties and events. I wondered what Lana was thinking as she sat across from Crosby this morning though. She had no idea that I had seen her kissing both him and Chip separately. Was she dating one of them and sleeping with the other? Whatever she was up to she had yet to share that with me or Luke. To date, our business together was just business, not personal, and that was fine by me. The less we were involved in each other's bedrooms the better.

"We have fewer weddings in autumn, but we still have

some important events coming up," I noted. "Secret Sunday, of course, and then we have Barry's party on election night."

"He's got my vote," said Crosby.

"Me, too," said Sam.

"Thanks guys, I know he appreciates that. Right now, it's a tight race. All we can do is get the word out and hope for the best."

Lana and I finished up the arrangements with the chef and then returned to our desks. A few misdirected letters had been sent back to us from Europe. So far nothing had panned out.

"Daddy is livid with Lloyd," Lana told me. "He's talked to everyone at his club, but they are all such cowards."

"In a way I understand them," I said. "They're afraid of losing their way of life."

"That's called progress."

Lana continued to surprise me.

The office phone rang. "The Duke, this is Derek. How may I help you?"

There was silence at the other end, then a faint clicking noise followed by an echo.

"Hallo? Sorry," the voice said, finally. "I don't make international calls very often." The accent was sing song-y.

My eyes widened. "Sunny?"

"Ja," she breathed out.

...

"Listen, gentleman, I don't have much time. I'm on my way to another fundraiser at the Rotary Club."

Lloyd opened the door of the Barton Bank to me and Barry and we walked right in and took a seat straightaway. This time there was no offer of cocktails or a tour. There were clear lines drawn in the sand now. We were not here as friends. We were here on business.

"This won't take long," I started. "Thank you for meeting us at the last minute. We just came here to ask you one more time, as a gentleman. We would like you to retract the threats to the Secret Sunday and Bears' Club members. It's not seemly, Lloyd. Don't you want to win this above board? Don't you want a fair fight?"

He laughed. "Is there really such a thing? I mean, let's be honest. Of course, I would beat you without this little coercion of mine. But I do love the extra insurance. And it didn't cost me a thing. It was free."

"How can you feel good about yourself?" asked Barry. "How do you sleep at night knowing that you're cheating?"

"I am most certainly not cheating. How distasteful of

you to suggest that. You offend me. I am simply using the tools that I have at my disposal to ensure the ending that I desire. A 'happy ending,' you could say." He smiled to himself, amused by his little joke.

"Nothing we can say or do will change your mind?" I asked. Barry had been adamant that we play fair, not underhanded. I wanted to give Lloyd every opportunity to prove that he was a worthy adversary, and not just a lout.

"Nothing," he smiled, firm in his position. "Now if you'll excuse me, as I said, I do have a fundraising luncheon I must attend." He stood as if to quickly usher us out the door.

I remained seated.

"I didn't want to do this, Lloyd." I shook my head sadly. "We gave you every chance to make it right. I'm sorry. I really am."

I reached into my coat pocket, pulled out my cell phone and dialed the last number called. I put the audio on speaker, then placed it on the coffee table between us. It began to ring on the other end of the line.

"What on Earth are you playing at here? What kind of a game is this? I have asked you to leave."

The phone picked up.

"Hallo?" she answered.

"Hi, Sunny. It's Derek and Barry. We're here at Lloyd's

right now. You're on speaker." My heart began to pound.

Lloyd turned white instantly and his eyes betrayed his emotions. He walked slowly towards the table. "No," he said. "This can't be…" His voice trailed off.

"Ja, it is. Sit down," she ordered.

And he did!

"Lloyd, I will only ask you this once. Do you understand me?"

He nodded.

"I can't hear you," she said sternly.

"Yes, yes," he stammered.

"These people told me what you've done. Threatened your friends with exposure. This is not okay. You and I have an agreement, Lloyd. And I would hate to break that now, after so many years in détente. That would be a shame wouldn't it?" she pushed.

"Yes," he said, quietly.

"Good. Just as I thought. Now clean up this little mess of yours. I don't want to hear otherwise. Do you understand me?"

He hesitated, then looked at both of us with narrowed eyes and gritted teeth. He was somehow motivated with fear but clearly angry. Then just as quickly as the feelings had overtaken him, he wiped his face of all emotions save acceptance.

"Yes, of course. I'll get right to that."

"Good. I'm happy to hear. Oh, and one last thing. My payment was late this month. Don't let that happen again." And the line went dead.

Lloyd appeared to be holding his breath. I thought we had better leave before he threw up.

"Thank you for taking the time to meet with us today," I said as we stood to leave. "We look forward to a fair fight. Barry? Shall we?"

I grabbed my phone and we practically ran out of that door, holding in our laughter until we reached the street corner where we practically exploded.

"What does she have on him?" he asked me.

"I have no idea. But whatever it is, it must be a doozy."

12

LOSING MY MIND

Halloween was my favorite holiday and Tucker had the party of the year planned at Gaycare. I couldn't think of a better way to celebrate the fact that we had finally found a way to make Lloyd play fair. With Election Day just around the corner, these next two weeks were sure to be busy for all of us. It only took a few days from our visit at the Barton Bank for the calls of support to slowly start rolling in. Lloyd still had his team players for sure, but Barry's underdog status began to gain traction.

Luke and I met Tucker, Barry, and Chinois at Gaycare to enjoy a fun evening of drinks and drag.

"You're not afraid of performing as Beret tonight, with the election coming up next week?" asked Luke.

"Why should I be?" answered Beret. "I've been 'Barry Henry, candidate for mayor' for weeks, now. I need to let my hair down once in a while. I told Aisha I would not hide the real me and she agreed. The voters need to understand who they're supporting, and tonight they're getting Edna Turnblad realness!"

Beret and Chinois had planned a duet of "You Can't Stop the Beat" from *Hairspray*, and I could not wait. Beret had on a flowered housecoat with what felt like yards of pink marabou trim. Chinois wore the classic plaid skirt and an enormous black bouffant wig with a giant sparkling bow. One quick head turn, though, and she was liable to take out two or three bar patrons.

"You could knock out someone with that thing," I laughed.

"I've never had complaints about my head before," she teased.

"I love it all!" said Tucker as he roller skated out from behind the bar in full 1970s roller disco regalia to kiss his man. "Your Edna has me shaking and shimmying." His cutoff denim short shorts left so little to the imagination that they practically telegraphed his religion. "Who are you supposed to be?" he asked me.

I had thought that the black suit, plastic cigar and eye patch gave it away. "I'm Nick Fury. Head of S.H.I.E.L.D. From the *Avengers*?" Crickets all around.

"I thought he was black," said Tucker.

"I just wanted a good excuse to wear an eye patch and hang around with this hunk."

Luke smiled and flexed his biceps, highlighted and hugged by his skintight Captain America get up.

"We're doing it for our country," I giggled.

Gaycare had been a smashing success. Tucker's membership plan pulled in his regulars every night and created a buzz this town hadn't seen since, well, ever? No one here cared about gay or straight or bi or any categories. They just enjoyed the vibe, danced, drank, and celebrated life. By the time Beret and Chinois took the stage for their *Hairspray* number the place was standing room only. The crowd loved their performance, sang along with all the words, and showered the pair with singles.

"They're gettin' pretty good tips," someone said in my ear. I turned to see a smiling Chip standing beside me with Jett by his side. "Am I an exclusive at Secret Sundays, or can I start taking my act elsewhere?" he asked.

"You do you, Chip," I answered. "I only get you one Sunday a month. But I have the feeling your talents are being appreciated elsewhere already."

He smiled cockily. "What can I say? It would be a shame to waste what I was born with," and grabbed his crotch.

I shook my head and laughed. "What are you two doing here?"

"I came home for fall break," said Jett. "We gotta put these fake IDs to good use. Fletch paid good money for 'em. Plus, I gotta vote for your guy next week. I figure he could use all the help he can get."

"You could have voted absentee, you know."

"And miss a chance to go into a dark room and pull a lever for the man?" He and Chip turned to each other and high fived. These two were their own favorite idiots.

"Hey, Tucker," Chip called out. "Y'all mind if I take a turn on the pole?"

"Have at it," he yelled from behind the bar over the roar of the music. "All proceeds go to Barry's campaign, though." He pointed to a glass tip jar at the corner.

"You got it!" Without a second thought he pulled his shirt off, handed it to Jett, and jumped on stage to the delight of the dancing crowd.

"He loves the attention, doesn't he?" I said to myself.

"You created a monster, man," said Jett, laughing.

"How are things up in New York?" Luke asked him and reached over to give him a one-armed bro hug.

"All good. Well, as good as can be expected. I sent Fletch off to rehab. He was just too much for me to handle. He was basically sleeping days and partying all night. I have no idea how he kept his sales numbers up, but his job never complained. I guess they all liked a good party, too. When he woke up one morning naked in Central Park, I guess he figured he needed some help. He came home wearing a trash bag he pulled out of a bin. He must have showered for a full hour. I think that knocked some sense into him."

"Good for him," I said amusedly. "But he's still an asshole."

Luke took a deep breath but didn't say a word.

"Yeah, he is," said Jett. "But he's an asshole with a problem. So, I helped him. He's on a twenty-eight-day alcohol and drug free staycation upstate and I have the whole place to myself. Brandee drops by once a week to check on me. She's pretty cool, after all."

"I'm proud of you," said Luke, and placed his hand on his shoulder.

"If I didn't know any better, I'd say you actually listened to some of the stuff we tried to teach you," I said.

"Oh, get off it, y'all. I'm not asking for an award or nothin.' And trust me, I've still got my selfish motives. I've got the whole penthouse to myself now!"

He smiled that shit eating grin we both knew so well and then made his way over to the stage to watch the show, twirling Chip's shirt over his head and hootin' and hollerin.'

"The more things change," I said, shaking my head.

"He's done alright for a strange situation," said Luke. "His move to New York could have turned out a lot worse."

I nodded, but then noticed something wasn't right. "Chinois? Are you okay?"

She was sitting on a bar stool on the other side of Luke. Beret and Tucker were somewhere in the crowd glad handling for votes and donations. I knew she wasn't drinking because of her meds, but she looked even more tired than usual.

"Chinois?" I called out again.

She seemed to break out of her fog. She looked over to me, but then looked right past me and smiled.

"Bubbe," she said, her hand reached over and waved away an imaginary someone standing just over my shoulder. "Bubbe, I don't want to come inside yet. I'm still playing."

"I don't think she's okay," said Luke. "We need to get her out of here."

Before we could act, however, Chinois beat us to the

punch. She grabbed the attention of the entire bar by standing up and promptly falling to the floor.

■■■

This was my second time in so many months sitting in this damn emergency room waiting area, and it didn't smell any better than before. Tonight, it was chaos, however. Halloween in any town only brings out the worst in people. This wasn't where I had expected the night to end. Drag queens cut with words and not actual knives, after all. Here we were surrounded by countless naughty nurses, naughty elves, and even a naughty, sexy hot dog. There were black eyes, broken bones, and busted buns. If we hadn't been there for such a solemn reason, I may have actually found it fascinating.

"I feel like we're trapped in a zoo," said Tucker as he took in the spectacle.

"It's called life," Beret said. "Honey, can you skate down the hall and grab me a coffee? This place sobered me up quick, but some caffeine will help get me through it."

We waited for news for what felt like an eternity. Chinois had been taken in hours ago, but no one had come out to tell us anything. Beret was nervous, of course.

"I thought she was getting better. She told me she was fine."

"I don't want to scare you," I said, "but I think she may not be telling us the whole truth."

We felt a sense of dread. Not wanting something to happen doesn't make it not happen. No matter how hard we wished, Charlie would still have chronic HIV. Everything hinged on his T-cell count. It was sobering indeed.

"Mr. Henry?" a voice called out over the crowd.

"Here! Yes!" We gave up our seats in the midst of the chaos and rushed over to meet Dr. Goldman.

"How is he?" Beret asked furtively.

"Let me just put you at ease," he said. "Just a case of dehydration. These new meds can really take a toll on him. I need you to make sure he's drinking lots of water and getting enough bed rest. I know he likes the attention at Saul's. I've seen him there. He's not hard to miss," he chuckled. "He's great at it, but if he wants to stick around awhile longer, he is going to need to take a break for a bit."

"I'll do my best to convince him."

"You'll need to. He's a tough one, for sure. I'm going to keep him overnight for observation, but he should be good to go tomorrow. You can see him if you'd like, but not all of you. He needs to rest."

Barry looked at us and we all nodded quickly for him to go.

"By the way, you've got my vote," the doctor said as they walked through the doors together.

■■■

I was catching Lana up on our adventures from last night, both fun and not so fun. "Barry's so busy with the campaign right now that he can't really spend the day taking care of Charlie. We have just over a week to go before Election Day and we need him out kissing babies, shaking hands, and eating funnel cakes. Tucker will take the first watch today, but we'll have to come up with something. Charlie says he's okay alone, but none of us feel very good about leaving him unattended. What if something goes wrong?" I shifted gears to the party. "Everything started out great at Gaycare. We even saw Chip and Jett. Chip spent a good thirty minutes dancing on the pole. The crowd loved him."

She didn't react.

Come on Lana, give me something. Anything!

She ignored me and picked up her phone. "Hey girl," she started, "I hate to ask you this, but do you think Miss Addie could help us out with something? I wouldn't normally ask, but it's kind of a family emergency. Barry's friend Charlie needs a short-term caregiver. Just someone to watch him, fetch water, keep him company. No, nothing medical, just pills and stuff and maybe read to him. Yes, that's right. From Saul's. Yeah, she's larger than life. Oh, you will? Thanks, girl. You're a sweetheart." And she hung up.

"What did you just do?"

"You said you needed someone. Amber will ask Miss Addie if she can help out a few days a week in her spare time. You'll have to pay her in cash. She'll give you a call tonight."

"When did you get so soft?" This wasn't the Lana I knew. This was the Lana that Luke had always talked about, but I had never seen.

She looked me over and frowned. "Can you please make yourself a little more presentable? Sailor Fielding should be here any minute to discuss little Prairie's birthday party. She may just be turning six, but that little girl knows what she likes."

■■■

Barry and Tucker voted in person at Parkville High first thing in the morning on Election Day. Aisha pushed the image of both of them out to social media and the Very Barry app soon after the morning papers had arrived. Mom, Dad, Luke, and I were there to support him. Tucker used his own Gaycare app to message all of his private bar members and remind them to get out and vote, hangovers be damned.

"How do you feel?" he asked Barry. "Just think, this time tomorrow you could be the mayor-elect!"

"I'm scared shitless," he said, his teeth barely separating as he smiled for the cameras. "What happens if I win?"

"Free ice cream for everyone!" said Tucker. He held his hand and they walked through the crowds shaking hands and chatting up the townspeople.

"This is like an alternate reality," I said to Luke under my breath. "I would have never imagined this."

"Oh, everyone loves Barry. They always have."

He was right. Though he could have a sharp tongue, my uncle always had a gentle heart. Even at his most bitter in the years before he met his boyfriend, I still loved spending time with him. This post-Tucker Barry was more alive than ever. He had discovered that he wasn't half as bad as his own negative press.

"How's it working out with Miss Addie?" asked Luke.

Barry had moved a rocking chair into his old room where Charlie was now staying. Miss Addie spent hours reading to him or doing her crossword puzzles once he drifted away to sleep. She had been such a help in the past week leading up to the election when Barry could not be at home as much as he wanted to. Amber was very gracious in freeing up Addie's time, and Addie returned the favor by preparing plenty of meals for her in advance. Amber couldn't boil water, but her husband Todd was pretty handy with a microwave.

"He's a real keeper," Amber said without a hint of shade.

"I'm actually a little worried about Addie," I said. "She's spending a lot of time running back and forth between her place, Barry's and Amber's. We need to step up and give them all a break after this week."

"Good idea," said Luke. "But first, let's hope he wins this election. Surprisingly, I think Barry's star is on the rise."

I agreed. I just hoped Lloyd hadn't planned any other underhanded crap we didn't know about.

■■■

Barry's election night party at the Duke was in full swing. Lana had Sam and Crosby rig up a balloon drop in the rafters. They had to use a cherry picker to get up high enough and thread a giant see-through fishnet from one end of the main salon to the other. She really could get men to do anything that she wanted. The polling stations closed at 8:00, but the networks had journalists in place outside the Duke ready to announce their projections as soon as they were in. Rumors were flying like crazy. The polls had varied so much in the last week that it really was anyone's game at this point. Lloyd's party was over at the country club, of course. Aisha had all the phone numbers and speech variations at the ready, depending on the outcome. Would Barry be calling to concede? Or would he await Lloyd's congratulations? We were all on pins and needles. I had been on a lot of stages over the course of my life, but politics were more terrifying than anything I had ever encountered, including that horrific production I saw of *Bring It On: The Musical* on Broadway. Lin-Manuel Miranda didn't talk about that one very often. I didn't blame him.

"Here's to Barry," I said, raising my glass. We were surrounded by our dear friends and family. "I'm sure none of us in a million years would have ever imagined that we would be here right now, awaiting election returns together."

"I'm so grateful to all of you," gushed Barry. "But especially you, Tucker. I've really upended our lives and you've taken it all in stride. I just want you to know I really love you. I will never be with anyone else. So that means if you leave me, I *will* die alone."

"You always say the sexiest things." He kissed him on the cheek.

"And Aisha, I could not have done this without you. No matter what happens, you're one of us from now on. I was not the perfect candidate by far. You made this lump of clay into something passing as a candidate. Thank you so much."

"It was my pleasure," she said. "At least you didn't have to threaten people with exposing their secrets to get their vote, right? We did our best and I'm proud of you. And we're not at the finish line yet, right?"

We held our glasses high and cheered, "Team Barry!"

Aisha pulled me to the side. "It's almost 8 o'clock. The projections will be coming in soon. I'm going to get him positioned near the stage so we can jump on at a moment's notice. The news cameras are all set up on the balcony. Is everything ready with the balloon drop? Just in case we have something to celebrate I want to make sure we get a great shot for the press."

"Sam's pulling the string," I said. I looked over at the bar and he wasn't with Crosby. We didn't have time to search all over the Duke for him. I reached down for my phone to call him, but then I remembered I had left it on my desk to charge. "We have like ten minutes. I'm running up to the office quick to get my phone. I'll be right back."

I pushed my way through the crowd and bound up the steps two by two. The door was locked as usual, but I was ready with my keys. What I wasn't ready for, however, was the sight of Lana sitting on her desk, her arms wrapped around yet another guy.

Oh, Sam! Not you, too?

13

TWO TRIBES

This time she couldn't pretend not to see me.

"Get out of here! *Now!*" she shrieked.

I scrunched my face together and slammed the door shut. *Shit!* I had no choice but to reopen it swiftly, but this time I kept my eyes closed.

"Sorry! Sam, balloon drop. *Now.*" I quickly pulled it shut again and rolled my eyes to the heavens. Chip, Crosby, *and* Sam? I was all for empowerment, but this was ridiculous.

Aren't you being a little greedy, Lana?

I didn't have time for this. I turned to head back down

to find Aisha when the door behind me opened and Sam appeared and smoothed his hair. I just shook my head as he followed me down the stairs. I rejoined Aisha and my family at the side of the stage as Sam crossed over the salon and up to balcony to be in position for the balloon drop. Barry had already taken the stage and was addressing the crowd, thanking everyone in attendance for their love, encouragement, and support.

"I am certainly not an establishment candidate," he said. "My campaign manager even suggested at one point that we bring back the Whig Party." Everyone erupted in laughter. "We didn't do that, but we definitely did this my way. You've seen the real Barry Henry in the last few weeks leading up to tonight. Wig or no wig, win or no win, I promise you this; I'll always wear a fabulous shoe. That's a guarantee from me!"

The crowd roared its approval. Aisha stood next to me; her phone pressed hard against her ear.

"Barry!" she called. "Barry! It's for you."

She jumped on stage and handed him her mobile. The crowd hushed as we raptly followed every emotion in his face.

"This is Barry Henry," he spoke into the receiver. "Yes. Yes, please. Really? You're certain? Thank you for calling." He smiled, then held the phone down. My heart was pounding out of my chest.

"That was the election committee," he said, addressing the crowd. His face broke into a broad smile. "The results are in. *We won!*"

■■■

The celebration raged on into the early hours of the morning. Parkville had never seen anything like it. Business suits mixed with the burgeoning LGBTQ community that Barry and Tucker had fostered. Pensioners mixed with students. The staffs from Saul's, Cochon's, and the Tater Tot all partied together. There were no rivalries here tonight. Lloyd, to his credit, called Barry to concede the election.

"He would have never done that had there not been a camera on his face," Red told us later.

I had to agree. Lloyd had tried to wage a bitter, underhanded campaign. Barry showed us the way. We fought fair, but we used everything we had at our disposal. Now it was my turn to reach out. I didn't know Sunny, and I initially felt bad about pulling her into in this mess, but I felt she should know that her involvement had paid off. I fired off a quick text message telling her that Barry had won the election and thanked her for her help. The message was delivered, but she didn't respond. I didn't expect her to write back and I certainly didn't hold it against her. She had left Parkville behind for a reason and that was really none of my business.

We shut down the Duke and made our way to our cars, hugging each other in the parking lot before we went our separate ways.

"What a great ducking night!" said Tucker.

"*Ducking?*" Barry sneered.

"I figure I need to clean up my speech," he explained. "I'm the Mayor-elect's boyfriend, after all."

■■■

The weeks seemed to race by after the election. Work, events, parties, and nights with our friends all blended together into one cozy memory. Thanksgiving night arrived and Luke and I stopped by Barry's place to pick him up on our way to the Walcott's dinner.

"How's it going in here?" We peeked our heads into Charlie's room to check in on him. He was sleeping, but Miss Addie looked up from her crossword puzzle and smiled. "Are you holding up?" I asked her.

"Just fine, just fine," she assured us. "Mr. Charlie is sleeping now. He's a tough one though. Don't you worry about him. He's still got the fire. He's keepin' me on my toes."

"I have to keep *someone* in this town interested in me," he said, rousing from his sleep. "I don't want you to forget me."

"Not a chance of that," I said.

Miss Addie stood up and offered him a glass of water. "It's time for your pills anyway. I'll be right back." She excused herself.

"We hope you're feeling better," Luke offered. "You really gave us a good scare at Gaycare."

"How rude of me for not yet thanking you for carrying me to the car," Charlie said. "I heard you were good with bodies, but now I have firsthand knowledge."

So much for our secrets.

"When duty calls," he said smiling.

"We're happy you're on the mend," I said. He did look better. "Any requests we can bring you back from Thanksgiving dinner?"

"No, I've had enough nights with turkeys in my life. I think I need to go vegetarian if I'm going to continue past my sell-by date."

"We'll let you rest," I said, as Miss Addie walked in with his medications.

We returned to the living room to push Barry and

Tucker along. They were running behind getting ready for the evening. To celebrate Barry's win, Red and Rosa had invited the entire Walter/Henry family over, including Tucker, to share a Thanksgiving dinner. For such a seemingly confident guy he was surprisingly nervous.

"You'll be fine," Barry assured him. "It's not like they'll take a disliking to you and make you wait outside."

"Please don't tell me I have to sit at the kid's table."

"There *is* no kid's table," I said shaking my head. "It's a mansion. The table in the main dining room seats like twelve people."

"Main? How many dining rooms are there?"

"Don't freak him out," said Luke and turned to assure Tucker. "It's not that big. You'll be fine."

"That's what all the men say." He flashed a devilish smile.

"We're in ducking trouble," deadpanned Barry and we all laughed.

We walked outside and the smell of lit chimneys from the neighborhood filled the air. Luke was our driver for the evening and the four of us got into his Jeep for the short trek over to the house.

"Is Lana bringing a date?" I asked Luke, stirring the pot. I couldn't resist. We had had a long discussion about his sister's secret trysts with Chip, Sam, and Crosby. Luke pushed me to leave it be until Lana decided to initiate the conversation. I had promised to keep my mouth shut, but the gossip was so good that I was having a very hard time containing myself.

"Is she dating someone?" asked Barry.

"*Someones*," I said, teasing.

Luke shot me a stern look from the driver's seat and I just giggled.

"Well she's gorgeous," said Barry. "I say let her do whatever she wants."

"Yeah, if she's got game there's no shame in that," said Tucker.

"Enough." Luke silenced us. His deep voice reminded us to behave as we pulled into the circular drive at his parents' house. "It's like having kids," he said to himself.

"But you said we get to share the same table," laughed Tucker. "You promised!"

We were running a bit late and I could see Mom and Dad's car was already here. Bammy and Michael, too. Luke rang the doorbell and we waited impatiently.

"Why can't we just go in?" whispered Tucker, but we all ignored him.

"Welcome!" said Rosa as she pulled the door open to reveal a wonderland of themed décor. "Happy Thanksgiving! So happy you could join us."

The front table in the foyer featured a giant arrangement of orange and yellow flowers with mini pumpkins and gourds.

"It smells fantastic, Rosa," I said as we took off our coats.

"Do I smell churros?" asked Tucker.

She smiled at him knowingly. "You must be Tucker. I've heard about you."

"Barry has a hard time not talking," he teased.

"We non-family members have to stick together," she said. "Why don't you join me in the kitchen while I finish up a few things? The churros just came out of the fryer."

"Dessert before dinner? You *have* heard about me!"

She reached for his hand and they walked down the hall together. The rest of us joined the others in the parlor. Red was standing at his usual place in front of the mantelpiece. The imposing oil portrait of his deceased wife Posy had been replaced, surprisingly, with a recently commissioned portrait of Red and Rosa. In it, Red was seated in a grand, leather tufted chair, Rosa standing beside him smiling, her hand on his shoulder. They looked good up there.

"And that is when I turned to the gentleman and said, 'One will not do. I want them all. Name your price.' He did, I accepted, and that is how I came to own the entire row of townhouses." He laughed at his little joke. Red's life was a game of Monopoly. I was grateful that none of us had the misfortune of landing on his wrong side.

"Welcome to the victor!" he exclaimed, directing a cheer to Barry. "I assume you know how to take care of yourself at the bar cart?" he asked, pointing to the dazzling array of liquor bottles at our disposal.

"Hello, old friends," Barry said, his mouth in a wide smile. "I was referring to the liquor, not you."

We kissed our way through the room.

"I'm so sorry we couldn't be at your party," said Bammy, holding her stomach. "I'm fit to burst. Everything's fine, I'm just over being the size of a Halloween pumpkin."

"We have just about a month to go for our Christmas baby," said Michael.

"I love how he says *we*," she laughed.

"The baby's room is ready at our house and Rosa has prepared a second nursery here. I'm a little nervous, but we're ready for this." He was clearly in love with the thought of being a dad.

"You're gonna do great," Luke assured him. "And if you ever need a break, we can take over for a night."

"Yes, just hand that little baby over to the guncles!" I exclaimed. "I've never even had a dog. What could *possibly* go wrong?"

"Did you just compare my baby to a household pet?" Bammy said aghast.

"Don't worry," Luke promised. "I'll keep this one at a safe distance. He's an only child, but he can learn. I was pretty good helping out with Lana when we were kids."

"Did I hear my name?" she asked as she approached with a martini in hand.

"I'm just telling them that I was a pretty decent older brother. I can handle a baby."

"True. If you can handle me and Derek you can pretty much handle anything," she agreed.

"Juggling skills must run in the family," I said, and took a sip from my cocktail.

Lana shot me daggers and I decided to step away before she changed her mind about liking me. I left them to continue with their baby talk and I joined my parents in the other corner of the room. Dad was telling Barry about his upcoming exhibition.

"I'm really excited about these new works. We're having an opening next week at Kit's gallery. I know you'll be busy with your mayoral duties, but we'd love it if you could attend."

"Oh, right now the city council is temporarily running the show. I don't get sworn in until January. I'm just meeting people, taking meetings, making plans. It's all very *House of Cards*. I'm hoping for a hot bodyguard."

"Just don't cause a scandal," my mom teased. "We know you'll do a great job. We're all so proud of you."

Rosa entered the room with Tucker in tow and invited us all to find our seats across the hall at the table. Dinner was about to begin. Lana, Bammy, Michael, Luke, and I took one side with Mom, Dad, Barry, and Tucker facing us. Red and Rosa sat at either end, with Rosa closest to the door so she could easily communicate with the servers. She preferred to be very involved with the cooking, but Red insisted she take a break and enjoy the meal. They had staff to wait on us, and he quite liked the ceremony of it all. The food began to arrive on large platters, and everything smelled wonderful. I smiled at my boyfriend and he held my hand tightly. It was such an experience to have all of these diverse parts of our lives together in one room. It was also nice to relax after the crushing workload of the past few weeks. Between the campaign and the events at the Duke, I had hardly had any time to breathe. We had eaten our way through the many dishes on the table when the pies and cakes began to arrive.

"Rosa, you are definitely going to be one of my favorites" said Tucker, and she laughed graciously.

"We are glad you are enjoying yourself," said Red.

"Barry speaks so highly of you. You have certainly brought out a better side of him."

"I don't *have* a bad side," said Barry. "There's just bad lighting."

"In any case, Rosa and are most pleased to host all of you here this evening. Elections, art galleries, football games, and an upcoming grandchild. Our lives are blessed indeed. I would like to raise a glass to toast all of you. Every one of you has contributed to our greater enrichment, and today we are thankful to recognize the love between us. Happy Thanksgiving."

"Happy Thanksgiving!" we said, glasses clinking.

"And in the presence of all of you I would like to make an announcement. Though Barry has truly led the way in showing us that a third act in life can bring many surprises with it, I have viewed the subsequent happy moments of the last few weeks as a warning to myself. I have spent so many years toiling away, in pursuit of the things that I had hoped would bring me joy. I am a provider, a man who has a sole need for ensuring the happiness and survival of his offspring. Luke, my first born, I am very proud of you, son. You have become a role model for the youth at the high school, and you continue to lead as you see fit, following no one's path but your own. You have found love, and I have no doubt that your future with Derek will be adventurous. Lana, you have conquered one industry and have now expanded into a second. Your charm and grace have carried you through from one success to another. You continue to surprise me, and I can only imagine that whatever you decide to pursue next will be successful. Michael, you are a new addition to our family, with your lovely bride-to-be at your side and a child on the way. You have chosen to create a place for yourself in the family real estate business, learning the ropes and detailing a clear vision for the future." He paused to collect himself. "I have spoken privately with Rosa, Luke, and Lana, and taken their wishes and advice into consideration. I would like to enjoy my golden years, spend time with my grandchild, and explore the world with my lovely wife. A formal announcement will be released on Monday, following the long holiday weekend, however I am pleased to share the news with you all right now. Congratulations to you, Michael, the new CEO of Walcott Properties." The room erupted in applause, hugs, and congratulations.

"You knew about this?" I turned to Luke and he winked at me. I was grateful that Red had included him in the discussion. I was surprised about Lana though. She had given us so much grief last year about wanting the lake house for herself. Then again, that was back when she hated me. Funny how times had changed.

JORDAN NASSER

"You're sure you're okay with this?" Michael asked Luke, as if he had read my mind.

"I have no interest in Father's company. He's always been aware of that," Luke assured him. "I'm very happy for you, and we all know you'll do a great job."

"I agree," said Lana. "I told Daddy that I wasn't into selling dirt. I enjoy what I do and I'm grateful that he has someone he can really trust to make sure it all runs smoothly. Besides, I have enough on my plate." She looked at me, daring me to speak. It took everything in my power to hold my tongue.

"Shall we all retire to the parlor for an after-dinner drink?" asked Red.

Lana was really pushing me to ask about Sam. She must have suspected or even known that we also knew about Chip and Crosby. But Luke was right. Until she initiated the conversation, I needed to stay out of it.

We had just settled into our places in the parlor when the doorbell rang.

Red looked at Rosa. "Are we expecting anyone else?" he asked.

She shook her head no. "I'll see who it is." She got up from her chair, opened the sliding pocket doors and walked to the front door.

We heard voices in the hall and resumed chatting

204

amongst ourselves. Rosa reentered the room with a stranger, a woman I had never seen before. Or had I? There was something strangely familiar about her eyes.

"Red, there is a woman here to speak to you. Sunny Barton." She stepped aside to reveal the mystery woman.

What was she doing here?

My dad looked as though he had seen a ghost.

"Stevie?"

14

THROUGH THE FIRE

Sunny Nyquist Barton was Stevie Ray Walter?

My dad leapt to his feet and grabbed Sunny in his arms. No one in the room was quite sure how to process their confusion.

"Stevie!" he cried. "Stevie, I'm so sorry. I'm so sorry."

My mother moved quickly to his side to console him.

What was happening?

Sunny continued to hug him as her eyes danced around the room. Barry looked stunned, Red was pale, and Bammy looked as confused as ever.

"What the *hell* is happening here?" she whispered to no

one in particular.

I looked over to her with wide eyes. For once even I was at a loss for words. Dad and Sunny broke their embrace and held each other at arm's distance, taking each other in from head to toe. Dad could not stop crying and Mom had her arm around him for support. Barry, like me, remained seated. He looked absolutely frozen with shock. Tucker watched everyone's faces with fascinated amazement. You could tell that he knew this would be an eventful night.

"Good evening, everyone. I'm Sunny Nyquist Barton." Sunny broke the trance and spoke, her voice carrying a hint of an accent. She stood at the entrance to the parlor for all of us to see. Dressed head to toe in shades of grey, black, and white, she immediately reminded me of a Scandinavian version of Diane Keaton. Her shoulder length light blond hair was streaked with grey. Long bangs danced just above her eyes. Her white blouse was slightly open, but not too revealing. She wore a silver statement necklace that looked like an amulet or breastplate protecting her chest. A large grey cashmere shawl covered her arms and traveled down to meet her black wool trousers. Her black leather boots were stylish with a sensible heel. Though she was clearly a woman of a certain age, her figure looked fantastic. Whatever she was doing, she was doing it right.

"Forgive me for intruding. I suppose I should have announced my intention to travel, but I was nervous. I wasn't sure I would go through with it, to be honest. I had vowed never to return, and here I am." She held her arms out palms up and laughed to herself a little.

"Stevie, I can't believe it's you," said my dad.

"I'm not Stevie," she corrected him, shaking her head. "I'm Sunny. I know this is a lot."

"I am so confused," Bammy said, speaking for all of us.

"It's called deadnaming," said Tucker, explaining to us all. "He's deadnaming her. I'm sure it's strange for you," he said to my dad gently. "When a person transitions, it's the proper thing to do, to call them by their preferred name. She's Sunny now. We should all call her Sunny."

"That's right," she said. "Thank you. I haven't had to explain this to anyone for years. I'm so used to being me now. This is my life."

"But I don't even know who Stevie is," said Bammy, "let alone Sunny. No offense, ma'am."

"I see," said Sunny. "This is a family gathering, so I can speak freely, no?" She looked to Red for guidance.

"Yes, yes of course." The words caught in his throat. He was still standing by the mantelpiece, but vocalizing seemed to break the spell that had frozen him. He sat slowly in his leather chair. "Please, have a seat," he said to her.

Dad rejoined Mom on the couch and Sunny took a chair of her own at the entrance to the room. Bammy wanted answers, and our visitor appeared ready to bring the truth. She crossed her legs and surveyed our faces. How strange it must have been for her to see Johnny, Barry, and Red after all these years.

"I'm not sure where to start. They always tell you to begin at the beginning. Here we go." She smiled and shook her hair softly, her right hand moving up to adjust her bangs out of her eyes. She held on tightly to the arm rests and took a deep breath before starting. "I was born Stevie Ray Walter. I was Johnny's older brother. But from the moment I can remember, I never felt at home in my body. I didn't have words for it, and I didn't feel as though I could explain it if I had tried. I just knew that the person I saw in the mirror was not the person I knew to be inside of me. Growing up I had no access to understand what was happening to me. I only knew that I should keep it to myself. That it was wrong. That *I* was somehow wrong. I knew I wasn't gay, or at least I didn't feel gay. That word didn't feel right for me, and besides, coming out as gay was not something I could have done, either. Maybe it would have been easier than trans, but I knew in my heart that the easy way was not going to be my path. My parents were loving. I never felt that they wouldn't love me. But I knew in my heart that they would never understand. My dad was busy with the farm and my mom cautioned me to ignore the taunting and teasing. I can't remember a time when I wasn't picked on by my classmates. I figured it was my cross to bear and I had to accept it. I learned to keep my feelings buried inside. That seemed to work for me. I became the quiet one, the strong and silent type. Then puberty hit and all hell broke loose. My body started going through changes that I didn't like. Changes that I didn't want. The reflection in the mirror was becoming what they wanted of me, rather than the me I knew I was. The bullying increased, even from you, my little brother." She looked at my dad. "That hurt, but I knew you were just going along with the crowd. I forgave you years ago, but I'm getting ahead of myself. Where was I?"

"Bullying," Tucker prompted.

"Yes, thank you. The bullying was bad, but still I pushed through it. I became angrier, I put on the façade of the straight, white male so that everyone would leave me alone. I was determined to leave this town after high school. That's the summer I met you, Red. You, Edward, Lloyd, Barry, you became my friends. We shared a connection. I wasn't sure how to explain it, but I felt like you all accepted me as the person I was. When Barry suggested a drag show for the fun of it, I thought he must have read my mind. Was he like me? The Glama Gals were born. Looking back, we were all so young, so naïve to imagine that we were just having a laugh. For me it was real though. It wasn't a joke. When we put on our shows I didn't want to change back into Stevie. I wanted to be that woman I then saw in the mirror. The hair, the makeup. She shone so brightly. I didn't want her to leave my life. I wanted her to *be* my life. But Edward got in the way of all of that. I knew I was attracted to him. Everyone knew, I could no longer hide it. I followed him around like a puppy dog. He made me feel so brave. The love I felt for him wasn't real love. I know that now. But at the time I thought he was my future. I fantasized about being his wife, the woman he came home to after a hard day at the office. I knew that I could offer that to him. I was so misguided. I should have never tried kissing him. My fatal mistake. When he hit me, my whole world crashed in. I was discovered. Exposed. I had set myself up for a lifetime of ridicule. And you didn't console me." She looked straight at Red, and then Johnny, and Barry. "None of you. Not one of you offered support in any way. *But Lloyd did.*"

We all sat straight up in our chairs, hanging onto every word she spoke.

"After Edward exposed my secret desires, I wanted to die. He didn't want me for who I was, and I knew there was no place for me here. I wanted to run. I was heartbroken. Lloyd tried to comfort me. I didn't care for him when I first met him. He was callous. Another spoiled rich boy who could have whatever he wanted. But now he wanted something he couldn't have. *Me.* And I realized I suddenly had a choice. Edward was the man I wanted, but Lloyd was the man I could get. It all happened very quickly. Lloyd insisted we keep everything quiet. It was very difficult for me. In public, I was outwardly ostracized. In private, he wooed me. He wanted to be everything to me that Edward detested. I was angry at him for keeping our relationship a secret, but my self-worth was so low that I was grateful to him for accepting who I was at the same time. I saw a different side of Lloyd. I saw who he really was behind that enigmatic smile of his. In that moment in our lives I understood him. We spent that summer together in secret. I confided everything to him. Told him I wanted to transition. I had contacted a hospital in Denmark that was well-known for many successful gender reassignment surgeries. I had no real money to speak of. I had barely saved enough for a bus ticket out of town. When Lloyd offered to cover all of the costs, I jumped. I didn't even hesitate. All I saw was the light at the end of a very long tunnel I had been traveling in since I was a child. We agreed that I would go to Denmark and have the surgery. I left without so much as a goodbye to anyone, save him. Lloyd set me up with an apartment in Copenhagen, and I began the process. Though I knew my surgery would be months or possibly even years away, I started living as 'Sunny.' I chose that identity because I finally felt happy. 'Nyquist' came later. It means 'new branch.' Sunny Nyquist was a fresh, new start for me. Lloyd and I sent letters. We spoke often on the phone. I told him everything that I was going through. My outside slowly started to match my inside. I found my look, my style. The hormones brought out my curves and I worked to alter my voice, as best as I could. The accent was an accident. I picked up the Danish lilt from my surroundings without realizing it. I hadn't really understood what I was about to endure though. The physical and mental weight of a transition is enormous. I mourned the death of Stevie, and then celebrated the birth of Sunny. I was disconnected from everyone in my past, except for Lloyd. He was the only one I would let in. It took years before I agreed to see him in person, before I agreed to become his wife. He asked me over the telephone, and I said 'yes.' We had fallen in love throughout this transition. I owed him everything, I really did. Looking back, we were both so naïve, though, to expect for me, Sunny, to be able to love the Lloyd that he was then. I wasn't the only one who had changed in those years, after all. It was stupid of us to think otherwise. Coming back to Parkville was terrifying. I couldn't see any of you. I didn't want to. I didn't know what you would think of me. And Lloyd? He didn't want to share me, and that was fine by me. He had his perfect wife locked up in his perfect estate by the river bend. It was yet another transition, but one I didn't ask for. I went from my own, free woman in Denmark to a pretty little bird trapped in a cage. No visitors, no friends, nothing. I remember Lloyd's parents sent a picture to the newspaper to announce that we had married. He flew into a rage. For months on end we rarely left the estate. He wanted to keep me for his very own, for his eyes only. It won't surprise you to tell you that I had other ideas. I didn't spend my life trapped in the wrong body only to correct that and end up a prized possession. We agreed that the persons we had become were not people who should be married to each other, so we decided to split. I wanted to leave town so desperately that we never even managed to get the divorce. We were probably never legally married anyway. Sunny Nyquist didn't exist in America. I flew back to Denmark, Lloyd offered to support me, and I agreed to keep quiet about that chapter of our lives together. He continued to send money, but our interactions slowly burnt out. We had been through the fire together, but we came out different people, and we no longer made sense as a couple. It was a small price to pay for the life I lead now." She readjusted herself in her seat and brought her hands together. "So, there we are. That brings us up to date, so to speak. Well, not entirely. I still live in Copenhagen. It's a very free, open city. I love it. I run a small boutique that carries hard to find sizes for ladies. *À propos*. I don't really think of Parkville, or at least I hadn't for years. Until one day out of the blue I received a letter from you, Derek." She looked pointedly at me. "I wasn't sure I should even respond. But something in me was curious. This life I had left had continued without me. Though I wanted nothing to do with the past it, it would be a lie to say I wasn't interested in the present. Speaking to you on the phone was emotional for me. I tried my best to hide it. Here was the nephew I had never known. What else did I not know? My mind exploded with ideas. When you told me what Lloyd was doing, threatening everyone in his club, I wasn't shocked. Lloyd likes his secrets. He always has. But I am tired of hiding for *him*. I lead my own life now. I was happy to be useful to you. After all of these years I had never once tried to find you online, but then suddenly it was all I wanted to do. When you won the election, Barry,

I had a little glass of champagne for you that night at dinner. But this life that you have all created! Drag queens and gay bars, politics and real estate. I was intrigued. I had let go of all of my fear and anger years ago. That was Stevie. But then I did something that even surprised myself. I must admit, I was impetuous. I booked a flight without telling any of you. I checked into a charming boutique hotel downtown. It's one of Lloyd's actually. I haven't been to see him yet. I can't quite bring myself to do that. But you, all of you, you are more interesting to me. I went to see you first, Johnny, but you weren't home. I then tried at Barry's place, and a very lovely lady named Addie was kind enough to direct me here. So, here I am." She paused. "What is there left to say, but Happy Thanksgiving?"

■■■

The next hour was spent trying to process everything that Sunny had told us. It was *a lot* to take in. Dad, Barry, and Red seemed to have the hardest time adjusting. I couldn't even imagine what it would be like for a close friend or family member to completely disappear then reappear again after decades, but as a different gender.

"That was out of this world fascinating," Bammy said

as we gathered in a huddle.

"Wasn't it?" Tucker agreed. "And she looks incredible. I mean, that Scandinavian vibe is *everything*."

I was quietly watching my family reconnect.

"Are you okay?" Luke whispered to me.

"Yeah, I'll be fine. I'm just blown away like the rest of you. I'm worried about Dad and Barry."

"He'll adjust," Tucker interjected. "He has a lot to share with her as well. I'm sure they'll have a good laugh, eventually."

"You think she'll stick around?" asked Luke.

"I don't know," I said, shaking my head. "I guess that all depends on Lloyd."

"It shouldn't depend on him at all," said Bammy. "She was clear on that. She's her own woman now."

"She's still taking money from him," said Luke.

"Why shouldn't she?" asked Tucker. "He didn't do right by her. I think she's owed that financial support, regardless of whether or not she keeps his secrets."

"I guess that's between them," I said. "And she'll have to face all of that sooner rather than later. Word spreads like lightning in this town. That's one thing that *hasn't* changed over the years."

■■■

We left our parents so they could have some private time with Sunny. She quickly pulled me aside at the door to have a word.

"I would like to get to know you better while I am in town, if that's okay for you?" she asked.

"Of course. No pressure though. I can only imagine how intense tonight has been. You know how to find me."

She smiled. She really was beautiful.

Gaycare was open tonight for the people who did not have Thanksgiving families. Tucker need to stop by, so he said goodbye to everyone and called his car service for a lift. Michael took a very exhausted Bammy home to rest. It felt like every night for her at the Walcotts was full of drama. Luke and I thanked Red and Rosa and then walked Lana out to her car to say goodnight.

"Well that was another doozy of a dinner, eh big brother?"

"Go big or go home, you know what I say."

"We do love our secrets, don't we?" I asked.

She narrowed her eyes. "Okay, *enough is enough*. I'm tired of your insinuations."

"What?" I was genuinely surprised. I wasn't trying to start a fight. We had been getting along so well. "I didn't mean anything. This town *does* love secrets."

"Oh, bullshit," she said. "You just want me to talk about *my* secret. And it's not that much of a secret anymore, since you busted in on me and Sam."

I started to object but chose to keep my mouth shut. Luke looked at me as if to say, *Wise choice.*

"But since you're so pushy, I'll tell you," she continued, "I *am* seeing him. *And* Crosby. *And* Chip. I've dated some pretty shitty men in life, so if I have three hot, eligible, attractive men who are interested in me, why should I choose? Who's to say I can't date all three? Are *you* gonna stop me?" She poked me in the chest with her finger. "*Are* you? Answer me!"

"No," I replied meekly.

"*And you?*" She poked Luke just as hard. "What about *you?*"

"No ma'am." He held his hands up.

"Good," she huffed. "Now that that's settled, y'all can leave me the hell alone. We just sat in there for a good hour listening to a precious soul tell us how hard love is. And you two, of all people, should understand where she's coming from. I don't need any shit from *either* of you tonight. You hear me. *Do you hear me?*"

"Yes!" we said in unison.

She unlocked her door, climbed in, and took off down the driveway without another word.

"What just happened? What did I say?" I asked

"Enough, apparently," he said, shaking his head.

15

THE POWER STATION

I had a restless night's sleep, no doubt due to the emotional evening we had just experienced. The next morning wasn't any better. We had barely had the time to process Sunny's arrival in Parkville when Barry called to tell us that Charlie had taken a turn for the worse.

"He's not okay," Barry said. "When I came home late last night Miss Addie told me she was concerned. He had labored breathing and kept calling out in his sleep. I called Dr. Goldman, but he suggested that it was better to let him try and rest through the night rather than move him. He's talking to his dead grandmother again this morning.

We're taking him in now. The ambulance is on the way. I'm scared, Derek."

"You did the right thing. We'll meet you there." I hung up.

"Charlie?" asked Luke.

I nodded solemnly

"Let's go," he said, and we hurried to get ready.

We had been to the hospital so many times this month that I thought we should invest in a parking spot. This was a place I didn't really want to keep coming back to, yet here we were again. We inquired at the information desk and Barry came out to fetch us. He and Tucker were in the room with Charlie.

"He's sleeping now," Barry said as he took his seat on the green pleather chair next to the bed.

Tucker was snuggled up against him on the armrest. They both looked as though they hadn't slept much. Charlie was on oxygen, the clear plastic mask covering his face. He had a needle taped to the back of his hand that led to an IV drip. He looked gaunt, but then again, no one ever looked good in a hospital bed.

"What did Dr. Goldman say?" I asked.

"They're running tests, checking his T-cell count. He's scheduled for a chest X-ray soon. He has lots of congestion. They're not sure yet if it's pneumonia or bronchitis. He's just on fluids now."

"How badly do we have to worry?" I asked, unsure if that was the right thing to ask out loud.

"I don't know, Nephew. We just have to give it time. I feel like he barely got here. We barely reconnected, and now this."

Tucker reached his arm over and tightened his grip on Barry as he began to get visibly upset.

"There's a reason he's here," I reminded Barry. "And that's you. He's here because he knows you'll be there for him. He chose you."

"Do you know how sad that makes me?" he asked. "He has no family or friends other than me? No one else who would step up and help? This is what happens to us when we get sick. We find out who are families really are."

Charlie began to cough. His eyes opened and he blinked several times.

Barry stood up and placed his hand gently on his arm. "Charlie? It's Barry. You're in the hospital, okay?"

Charlie took a deep breath, coughed again, then lifted the oxygen mask from his face slightly. "Really? I never would have known that from the smell and the overhead lighting. I'm sick in my lungs, not in my head. Though I did have some fabulous hallucinations. My bubbe wasn't really here, was she?"

"Yes, your grandma was here," teased Barry. "She'll be back soon. She just went down to the cafeteria to fill her purse with sugar packets."

"Oh, good. I hope she picks up a nice pair of salt and pepper shakers too. I don't care for the ones at your house."

"You're so weird," he laughed.

"But you always go along with it."

"Because you're my kind of weird." He shook his head. "It's nice to see you're feeling good enough to joke. You scared the hell out of us."

"Oh, I still feel like shit." He coughed again loudly. "My lungs feel like someone's sitting on them. He's about your size. I'd prefer it if you could find someone smaller, preferably a bit more my type."

"We'll see what we can do." Barry placed the mask back over Charlie's nose and mouth. "You need to keep this on."

Charlie breathed in the oxygen. "I heard you, you know, earlier. Talking about me. You're right, I have no one else. I've faced everything in my life with a mixture of cold feet and sarcasm. I know I'm a lot to deal with, but I had nowhere else to go. I've been alone so much of my life that I thought I was used to it. Then I changed my mind and decided I didn't want to die alone. Thank you. Really."

"Stop it." Barry's eyes started to well up with tears. "You're not going to die."

"Watch me." He closed his eyes and took another deep breath of the oxygen.

"You just be quiet." Barry continued to hold his hand.

I walked over to kiss my uncle on the cheek. "Let's give him some time to rest," I said.

"I need to wait for the tests and see what the doctor says." He shook his head, determined. "I'm staying right here."

"Call us if there's any change or if you need anything at all."

Luke and I left the three of them in the room and started back down through the hospital corridor. We were barely back at the car when my phone rang. All I could hear was panting.

"Bammy? What the hell?"

"*Baby!*" she screamed, followed by more panting and heavy breathing. "*Baby! Baby! Baby!*"

"Where are you? Are those sirens?" As if on cue the ambulance screeched into the parking lot at the emergency entrance. I looked to Luke and said, "It's Bammy!" We took off running, a pair of real-life ambulance chasers.

The attendants flung the doors open wide, and sure enough, there she was on a stretcher. Michael jumped out beside her, his hand tightly holding hers as they started to wheel her in the doors.

"*Baby! Baby!*" she kept screaming into the phone.

"Bammy, I'm right behind you!" I yelled. "We're here!"

We caught up with her stretcher and ran right beside them down the hall.

"*You're here! You're here! Baby! Baby!*" she gasped.

For whatever reason we were both still yelling into our phones. We reached the final set of double doors and the nurse stopped us, telling us we would have to wait behind.

"Bammy! You've got this. *You've got this!*" I kept screaming. Her phone went dead.

"Never a dull moment," said Luke.

■■■

We spent a full hour in the waiting room before Michael had the opportunity to come out and tell us anything. Everyone had shown up in that time: Red, Rosa, and the whole Scooby Gang.

Michael entered the waiting room, a look of relief on his face. "False alarm, everyone. Nothing to worry about. She's fine. Just Braxton Hicks."

"Braxton who?" asked Tommy.

"Braxton Hicks," Meredith answered. "False labor

pains. It's a tightening of the uterus."

I was glad I wasn't the only one. My studies of the female anatomy had never gone that far.

"Can we see her?" I asked.

"Just for a moment, and only a few of you at a time," said Michael.

"You two go," Kit reassured me. "Tell her we love her."

"Will do." I kissed her on the cheek then walked back with Luke and Michael to check on our girl.

Bammy's brow was wet with sweat and she was gripping the bed rails so tightly that her hands had turned ghostly white.

"I guess someone wanted some extra attention today," I said to her as we entered. "You didn't have to do all this."

"Trust me, not my idea," she panted. "I'm not ready for this." She looked panicked and nervous. "It's too early. The baby's not done yet."

"It's not a cake," I reminded her. "The kid will know when it's time to come out."

"Oh, really? You didn't."

I guessed I deserved that one. I smiled. "Well, he or she is just excited to see the world that is waiting for them. Look around. Who wouldn't want to be a part of this place?"

"I'm not ready," Bammy said on the verge of tears. "What if I suck at this? What am I gonna do? It's not like I can give up."

"You're not going to suck," Michael assured her. "You have plenty of love to give. We'll get through this together."

"But what if I don't know what to do? What if I do something wrong? What if I just can't deal with all the responsibility?"

"Bammy, you're running a school full of crazy kids," I told her. "You've put up with years of my foolishness. You've taken care of all of us when we've needed you. What you don't know, you'll figure out. I believe in you. We all do."

She threw her head back. "Fine. Just promise one thing."

"What's that?"

"The moment I have this child you'd better be right there waiting with a cocktail. I don't care if you have to carry a cooler of ice in your car for the next month. You just be ready. You hear me?"

"Loud and clear," I smiled. That was our Bammy.

We left her with Michael and walked out to get Red and Rosa next. They were very anxious to see Bammy and

Michael, even if the baby wasn't quite here yet.

"What a day," said Luke as we went back out to the parking lot for the second time that day. "We haven't eaten a thing all day. I'm starving. Should we head over to the Tater Tot for lunch?"

"Sounds good," I agreed.

As we opened the car doors, I saw yet another familiar face walking towards the hospital entrance.

"Miss Addie," I called out.

Luke looked behind his shoulder and spotted her as well. She half smiled at us and then paused, as if she had been caught doing something she wasn't supposed to do. She hesitated, then changed course, walking towards our car rather than the hospital.

"Hey, Miss Addie," I said. "Barry's inside with Charlie. He's in pretty bad shape. They think he may have pneumonia."

"Oh, yes," she said. "I should stop in and say hello, if he's up to it."

I cocked my head. If Addie wasn't here for Charlie, why was she here?

She read my mind. "I have other reasons to be here," she nodded.

"Are you okay?" asked Luke. "Is everything alright with you?"

Her face fell and we could see the sadness in her eyes. "It's not me," she sighed. "It's my sister, Mabel."

...

"Miss Mabel, I could kill you right now," I said to her as we sat by her hospital bed, my hand resting on hers.

"Oh, no need," she answered. "This cancer's gonna get me before you can."

"How long have you known? Why didn't you tell anyone?"

She smiled bravely and laughed. "Why you askin' me all that? What good's that gonna do? You here now, ain't you?"

Miss Addie had confessed in the parking lot that Mabel was terminally ill. She hadn't told a soul but her sister. The anguish was too much for Addie to bear alone anymore. I felt terrible because we had asked her to help out in the last few weeks with Charlie, when all this time she should have been by her sister's side.

"Mabel's tough as they come," she promised me. "She didn't want me there. I was just spinning my wheels. Taking care of Mr. Charlie actually helped me. Put me to good use. Don't you worry your mind 'bout that."

This was all too much. The pressure of the day finally

got to me and I felt the well of tears about to explode. Miss Mabel could see it in my face.

"Don't you do that," she said. "Your head's in the wrong place. I ain't dead yet. Don't think of the worst part of somethin'. It spoils the rest. We done had plenty of good times, ain't that right? You make sure to keep those."

She was right, indeed. We reminisced about our visits in the school office, that night I twirled her about at the school dance, and the moment she told me about her relationship with Barry's wife, my Aunt Janey.

"Don't you let them mess up my file cabinets. I done spent years keepin' everything in order. I shoulda trained someone new."

"There's no one who can replace you," I assured her.

"It ain't about that. It's not about how much time you got, it's about what you do with that time. If you take one lesson from me, let that be the one. You use that time that you got. Keep on goin' forward. All this lookin' back that you do gets you stuck in your mind. You keep that focus, you hear me? Now git. I need me my rest. Addie been driving me crazy tryin' to take care of me. 'Bout time I let her have what she wants."

I reached down and kissed her on the forehead. I just hoped it wasn't for the last time.

■■■

"I feel like we're stuck in *Groundhog Day*," I said to Luke as we made our way to the parking lot for the third time that day. "No matter what we do we can't seem to get out of here."

"I think we should run for it now, don't you?" he asked.

"Quick. Before someone else we know rolls up. I'm shot, emotionally. I need fried food. Stat."

We decided to stick with our original plan and head to the Tater Tot for some Southern comfort food. We asked the hostess for a table for two, but when she walked us into the dining area, we changed our minds.

"That's a friend of ours," he told her, nodding towards the corner booth. "We'll just join her." She smiled and he took the menus out of her hand. "Room for two more?" he asked as we approached the side of the table.

"Don't you know I prefer three guys?" asked a sneering Lana.

"I deserved that," I said, taking the seat opposite her. "But don't be mad at him."

"I'm not," she smirked. "I'm just not in the mood to play twenty questions today. Especially about my love life."

"I wasn't planning on going there," said Luke as he took the chair next to her. "How are you? Why are you all alone?"

"I needed some alone time. Some time to think." She took a sip of her drink. "Everything's fine, I just needed a breather. How's Bammy? Daddy said he saw y'all at the hospital"

We filled her in on Bammy, Charlie, and Miss Mabel.

"She reminded me that life was about what we do with it."

Lana looked at me and rolled her eyes. "Look, I know you're dying to ask. Let's just get it over with, okay?"

"Are you sure?" I was positively filled with glee for the first time that day.

"Shoot. Before I change my mind."

"*Three* of them? Three? How does that work?!"

"It's not like some wild orgy, if that's what you're thinking. You can just get that image out of your mind right now."

Luke blushed and shielded his face. "I don't know about this."

"I just like them all. Why should I decide? Crosby's smart. He knows a little something about everything. Sam is funny as hell. He makes me laugh. And Chip? Well, I'm sure you can imagine what he's good at."

"Oh, my lord," said Luke and looked to the heavens.

"Do they all know about each other?" I asked.

"At first, no," she confessed. "I was juggling them all secretly, trying to decide which one to go with. But they all make me happy in their own special way. First, I told Sam and Crosby because they're friends and I didn't want them to fight. Once they were clued in, I told Chip. He thought it was cool, of course. Then you guys found out and I kinda freaked. I don't want to tell Daddy. I don't think he'll get it."

"Your dad's seen a lot," I assured her. "I think you'd be surprised."

"I don't know. One day maybe. For now, I'm just having fun. It's not like I'm moving in with three men and starting a commune."

"Oh, I would pay to watch that show," I said. "Can you imagine Chip on TV? He'd never wear clothes."

Luke continued to shake his head. "Can we move on?" he pleaded with us. "I'd actually rather be back at the hospital than listening to this."

"Let's get you a beer," she said.

I smiled to myself. Lana wasn't asking for too much, she simply wanted what she deserved. I couldn't begrudge her that. It wasn't easy to find one person who was smart, funny, *and* great in bed.

Not everyone could have a Luke.

16

DO YOU BELIEVE IN LOVE?

Luke got the call first thing Monday morning. Bammy had been released from the hospital and was ordered to stay at home on total bed rest for the remainder of her pregnancy. The school board met and appointed him as Acting Principal of Parkville High School. He graciously accepted.

"Are you gonna call me to the principal's office, Mr. Walcott?" I asked with a naughty gleam in my eye.

"Get that thought out of your head right now," he laughed. "I'm gonna do this right."

"And you'll be great," I told him. "I'm proud of you."

With Mabel in the hospital the school board needed to hire a temporary secretary until the position could be permanently filled. They needed someone with good typing skills who was capable of office management and could handle a bit of chaos. My mom Audrey stepped right up.

"My husband's so busy with his art," she told the board. "Barry's going to be mayor, my son has his hands full at the Duke. I just want to be useful. I'd like to fill in until you come up with someone else."

The town of Parkville was starting to settle down as our crazier than usual autumn transitioned into winter. It was December 1st, World AIDS Day, and that fact wasn't lost on Barry.

"He doesn't seem to be getting any better," he told me on phone. "It's like he doesn't want to."

I was seated at my desk at the Duke pulling together our year-end numbers.

"Dr. Goldman says his pneumonia is beatable. He just needs to find the will to do it. I think he's given up."

"Then you have to help him find his mojo again. What will motivate him?"

He paused for a minute. "I don't know. I can't even think anymore. A hot guy?"

I turned my head and waved to get Lana's attention. "Hey, do you think Chip could help us out with something?" I asked her. "Barry says that Charlie isn't pulling out of his funk. He needs a feel-good if he's going to beat this thing."

"I'm on it," she said and picked up her phone. "As long as it's not a *feel-up*."

"We got this," I told Barry. "Chip could bring anyone back to life."

"Brilliant! Keep me posted, Nephew. Thank Lana for me!"

I hung up the phone. "It's kind of you to share him," I said to her.

"There's plenty of him to go around. A girl can't be *that* greedy."

"Have you ever heard the term *an embarrassment of riches?*"

As if on cue, Crosby knocked twice on our open door. He smiled furtively at Lana, then turned to me. "You have a visitor downstairs waiting for you. Sunny."

"Great, thanks."

To their credit, Sam and Crosby were still both focused on the Duke, not letting their relationship with Lana interfere with anything. I didn't think it was possible, but it seemed to be working out.

"Sunny and I are having a lunch date. See you soon."

"Ask her where she got that shawl for me, will ya?"

I walked downstairs to greet her and yet again her presentation did not disappoint. She wore a cream cashmere cowl neck sweater with an enormous off-white wool coat and a faux fur hat. She was pure *Dynasty* meets *Doctor Zhivago* fantasy.

"Wow!" I exclaimed. "You do know how to pull off a look."

"The best that Lloyd's money can buy," she laughed. "Are you ready?"

"I am. Let's go."

She had a car waiting for us outside. One of Tucker's, of course. She told me that she missed Southern comfort food, so I had booked a table at the Tater Tot. She was a beautiful woman who commanded attention, so it was no surprise to see that all eyes were on her when we entered.

"How strange is it for you to be back here?" I asked as we sat in our booth. "Is it uncomfortable?"

"Yes and no. It would have been awful for Stevie, but I don't mind it as much as I thought I would. Stevie was timid, afraid of who he was. I'm fairly straightforward. I know what I want. It's the new Scandinavian side of me I guess."

"May I ask, have you seen Lloyd?"

"Yes, of course," she smiled. "You know how it is, the more things change the more they stay the same. We have so much history, he and I. We actually love each other. We just can't live together. We're both too different now. *Literally*. We work better together at a distance. A great distance!" she laughed. "I thought he would be so angry with me interfering with his election nonsense, but he actually likes a strong, powerful woman. That's the thing with Lloyd. If you treat him as though he has the upper hand, he'll take you for all you've got. Just show him who's boss."

"Great advice. I'll keep that in mind."

"He's been divesting, but I guess you've noticed."

I mentioned that I had. "Money problems?" I asked.

"No, no. He had a little health scare. Nothing to worry about it turns out. But it was enough to make him realize what was important in life. We had no kids of course. He has no heirs. He has always loved his businesses more than any person and I think he just wants to see his 'children' left in the proper hands. So, while he has a say, he's letting them go. He may even visit me in Copenhagen. I'll make him stay in a hotel though. Otherwise I'd kill him for sure!"

We both laughed.

"Would you like to visit me one day?"

"I would. Absolutely!"

"I'd like that."

We enjoyed our lunch together and traded stories from our respective childhoods. There were so many things to catch her up on; a lifetime of memories.

"Your dad and I had a good cry. Lots of built-up anguish there. We are a family of runaways, aren't we?"

"Yeah," I scrunched my face. "But we also seem to come back to the scene of the crime."

"You're settled? You and Luke?"

"Yeah," I smiled. "I didn't think it was possible, but Parkville's home. We have a good life here. Good friends. Family."

"I'm still a loner. I can only handle friends in little doses."

"I get that. I used to think I was all that I needed. Now I know better. I'm just a small part of something larger."

"Well I'm happy to be a small part of your small part." She held up her glass and we toasted.

"To family," we said.

■■■

My cell phone was on vibrate, but it was loud enough to wake me up. I looked at the clock. It was just after 5 o'clock in the morning.

"It's gotten worse. You'd better hurry if you want to say goodbye."

Luke looked at me with sleepy eyes. He could tell by the look on my face that we needed to run.

I was too shaken to drive. He was better in situations like these. He parked the car and we raced through the parking lot, and then sprinted past the reception desk. We already had the room number memorized. Our bodies knew the way.

Miss Addie looked up at me with sad, tired eyes. "I've been up with her all night. It's time."

We sat by her bed, Addie, Luke, and me. Miss Mabel didn't have any other family. We were her family. We held her hands and soothed her as best as we could. She smiled softly but didn't speak. And then she was gone.

•••

Miss Mabel requested that her funeral be held at the Baptist church she had attended since she was a child. Though her faith did not always agree with her life, she made sure that her life was always filled with faith. That's just the kind of person she was. Luke made sure that every single staff member and student from Parkville High attended her celebration of life. The church hadn't seen attendance this great since they televised President Obama's inauguration. The audience was a sea of black suits and dresses topped off with elaborate hats, veils, feathers, and bows. Barry and I were both pallbearers. I had never cried so much in my life. I could barely see where I was going. I just knew that if I messed up, Miss Mabel would be back to haunt me, so I pulled myself together. In the receiving line, Miss Addie hugged me, and I almost lost it completely. Then she opened up her purse and said, "Mabel wanted you to have this." She handed me her little silver flask. Luke had to physically help me back to my seat.

The days that followed were a blur. Losing someone of Mabel's stature hit me hard. Bammy was still home on bed rest. She was so torn up that she couldn't attend the funeral. She wasn't due for another two weeks.

"I don't know what we'll do without her," she said.

"It won't be the same, that's for sure," I agreed.

■■■

Sunny flew back to Denmark as planned, but we promised to stay in touch.

"Maybe you can visit next summer," she said, "when

the sun never seems to set. You'll love it."

Barry called me as we were about to turn in for the night.

"Charlie's coming home tomorrow!"

Finally, some good news.

"Chip was amazing," he said. "That boy has some *talent* for sure. Not only did he revive Charlie's spirits, but he had the entire nursing staff on alert, and even a few of the doctors. I won't be surprised if we see a few of them at Gaycare soon. Tucker's going to build an evening around him. I hope that's okay?"

"Chip is his own man. I have no problems with that at all. Lana's the one you have to watch out for."

"From what you've implied she has a full plate of men. I have a feeling she won't mind letting him out of the coop occasionally. He really lifted Charlie's spirits. He's kicked the pneumonia. Dr. Goldman says he should still rest a bit before he gets back to work, but there's nothing to say he won't make it for years to come if he just takes care of himself. I think he just needed to find love. Not *love* love, but the kind of love that makes you understand your own value. You know what I mean?"

"I do."

We said goodnight. Luke was in bed next to me occupied with his phone.

"Everything alright?" he asked.

"Charlie's being released tomorrow."

"All hail the power of Magic Chip."

"*Magic Chip*. I have to tell Tucker that one. He'll love it. Who are you texting?"

"Bammy. School stuff."

"You've been on your phone a lot lately. I've never seen you so attached to it. What's up?"

"Like I said, school stuff. It keeps me busy. I love you."

"Don't distract me with love. That never works."

"How about kisses?" He tossed his phone to the side. "Will lots and lots of kisses do the trick?" He grabbed me in his strong arms and started covering my face with tiny kisses from my neck to my forehead, to both sides and back.

I tried to pull away and I couldn't stop giggling. Finally, he paused, and I spoke up. "You missed a spot."

■■■

Luke's new position kept him fairly busy. Recently he had so many late-night meetings that I ended up eating alone more often than I would have liked. I was feeling lonely and I wanted company, so I sat on the couch in our living room and called Tommy, Kit, my parents, Barry. None of them could talk and all of them had plans. I even reached out to Lana.

"Sorry. No can do. Crosby's making us dinner and Sam has picked out some movies for the night. Chip's coming over after his gig at Gaycare."

"You mind if I join you?"

"You've *got* to be kidding me. I'm pretty amazing but even three men is enough for me." She hung up.

I rolled my eyes.

Bammy. She won't let me down.

I called her for a video chat, and thankfully she answered right away.

"Oh, thank *God,*" she said. She held up her phone to show me her room. "I'm bored out of my mind. I'm so over being in this bed."

"It's an enviable position. Pillows, endless movies, a man serving you food. I could get into that."

"Not with a watermelon in your stomach pressing up against your bladder making you think you have to pee every ten minutes. Trust me, you couldn't."

She was right. "You're almost there. Two more weeks, right? How much time are you planning on taking off once the baby's born?"

"Well, I'm not even thinking about my job right now.

Luke's doing a great job. With Michael's work it's not like we need the money. I'm thinking of taking off the whole spring and summer. The school will live without me until next fall."

"Nice. I wish I could have a baby. I'd love the extra vacation."

"Honey, if you think having a baby is like being on vacation you got another thing coming. Maybe you two should start with a pet or something, first? *Oh!*" she winced.

"What?"

"Oh, nothing. Well, *something*. The baby kicked. Hard. *Oh!*"

"Are you sure you're okay?"

"I'm fine," she assured me, then screamed. "*Oh! Damn!* Oh, shit. Oh, no. *Oh no, oh no, oh no.*"

"Bammy?"

"Hon, I'm gonna need you to call an ambulance. My water just broke."

I stood up. "Are you serious? *Oh my god.* Oh, man. *What do we do? What do I do?*" I was panicked.

"Derek, snap out of it!" she said sternly. She then spoke to me very calmly and directly. "Hang up the phone. Call me an ambulance."

"You're an ambulance."

"Cute. But you're not doing me any favors. I'm getting my emergency bag and then unlocking the front door. Tell them I'll be waiting right inside, and they should just come in. I'm calling Michael. See you there." And she hung up.

Fourteen hours later little Mabel Faith entered the world a healthy, happy baby girl, albeit about a week earlier than planned.

"She wanted to do things her way," Bammy said from her wheelchair as we peered through the nursery window to see our little bundle of joy.

"She gets that from her mom," I said grinning.

"The doctor said she'll be fine. A few days in the hospital, then she'll be good to go. She just needs to get those lungs pumping."

Red and Rosa were on cloud nine.

"She has quite a colorful family waiting for her once she gets out," I said.

"Just imagine what the world will be like by the time she's a teenager," she said dreamily.

I looked down at her. "Are you still on drugs?"

"Major. They're *so* good. And I'm not sharing."

I pulled the silver flask from my pocket and held it up. "To Mabel," and took a sip.

■■■

"Derek! Hurry up! We don't want to miss the Christmas Eve concert," Luke yelled to me from the living room.

I was in the bathroom checking my final look in the mirror. "Why are you so into this damn thing?" I asked. "You always hated the choral stuff at school."

"I'm the acting principal. I have to keep up the façade, okay? Especially now that I have the position through the rest of the school year. Now get moving. I have the car already warmed up."

We drove to the old town square downtown. Thankfully we hadn't had any snow yet. The concert was planned for the outdoor stage, and the rows of white wooden folding chairs with padded pleather seats were surrounded by outdoor propane heaters. I liked the look of the little fires everywhere.

"Come on, I reserved places for us in the front row."

"Did you get seats for everybody?" I asked.

"Babe, I can't do everything. I'm sure they can all take care of themselves."

"This new job is making you kinda bossy."

He ignored me. We took our places and I scanned the crowd. I couldn't see Bammy, Kit, or Tommy. Not even my parents. It felt like I hadn't seen anyone for days.

"Just in time. It's starting," he said.

I didn't think I had seen him so excited since the big football game in the fall. The concert began sweetly enough with the kids' choir from the local church. Each group that took the stage was older than the one before, until we finally ended with the adult choir. The evening was actually more fun than I thought it could be. After their final song ended, I was shocked to see Barry come onstage in full Beret regalia with Chinois by her side. They both wore their glimmering, shimmering best.

"*Barry Christmas!*" he shouted as he came on stage. "Hello, hello! Thank you so much for coming out tonight and celebrating this fabulous holiday season with us," she said. "In the spirit of joy and love, I do hope you'll indulge us in a final little number we'd like to perform for you. 'All I Want for Christmas Is You!' I've asked a few friends to join me. I hope you enjoy it." He looked down at me and winked.

The opening chords started, and I began to laugh out loud like a little kid. One by one, everyone I knew came out from backstage to join the singing: Mom, Dad, Tucker, Bammy, Michael, Kit, Shawn, Lana, Sam, Crosby, Chip, Aisha, all the girls from Chesty Cheese. It was a stage full of love and laughter and friendship. A few of them carried large placards with images of wrapped presents, snowflakes, Christmas trees, and treats. It was amazing! Barry and Chinois commanded the stage, they had such presence. In the final notes, some of my friends and family came forward one by one and flipped their cards, holding them below their smiling faces. It didn't take long for them to spell out the words MERRY CHRISTMAS. The song ended and the entire crowd roared its approval. This must have been whey they were all busy! But why hadn't they included me? Before I could run backstage and congratulate them all on pulling off this magical hat trick, Barry and Chinois went to either side of the stage and held their arms out, welcoming one more player.

"Luke? What are you doing?" I asked as he stood up.

He left my side to join them onstage, then with his hands he tapped a few cards along the line. CHRIST and S flipped their cards back to images and stepped out of line, leaving just MERRY MA.

I didn't get it. Was this a mistake?

Luke saw my face and smiled nervously. He got down on one knee as the E and A quickly switched places.

It wasn't a question. It was a statement. In public, no less.

MARRY ME.

I froze. Everyone from the stage and all the townspeople in the whole square were staring at me, and for once, I didn't know how to act. Luke caught my eye and I found my way. I stood up, and the crowd grew silent.

"Yes!" I yelled at the top of my lungs. *"Yes!"*

■■■

We shut down the Firelight that night with the most raucous Christmas Eve party the place had ever seen. Luke had given me a beautiful silver engagement ring and I couldn't stop staring at it. It clinked on every glass I touched. I loved the sound.

"I love you," I told him for probably the millionth time that night.

"I love you," he repeated.

We kissed. A lot. We were surrounded by the friends who meant everything to us.

Bammy was sharing pictures of baby Mabel. "She's coming home from the hospital tomorrow. Christmas Day! I can't believe it."

"I want to talk about the wedding," said Meredith. "Where are you having it?"

Luke looked at me and shrugged. "We haven't talked about that yet. I'm sure Father and Rosa would love for us to have it at the house, if that's okay with you?"

"I think that's perfect." He could say anything, and I would have agreed at this point.

"You know, he pulled me aside on Thanksgiving, after he made Michael CEO of his company. He wants us to have the house. He and Rosa want to retire in one of those bungalows at the country club. That way he can wake up and be on the greens before anyone else."

"Seriously?"

"Yep. He even put his arm around me and said, 'One day this will all be yours,' completely unironically. I don't think he's even seen *The Lion King*."

I laughed so hard. I reached up and kissed him. One long, glorious, perfect kiss.

I heard Kit say next to me, "You know what's weird? Seeing Derek happy."

AFTERWORD

Through the Fire almost didn't happen.

When I completed writing *This Fire Inside*, the third book in the *Home is a Fire* series, I had a clear vision of walking away from the story of Derek and Luke with an open ending. My readers had other ideas. I am happy that you spoke up, and I hope you have enjoyed this fourth and final book in the series. Derek, Luke, Barry, and the rest will live on in our hearts. Until Netflix calls, of course.

For now, I have a few words of gratitude. Thank you, Eunice Chang, for taking on editing duty. Your eye caught many a misspelled word and poorly placed comma. I take full responsibility for any typographical or grammatical errors that remain.

Thank you, Patrik Nerséus, for taking my own original artwork and reimagining it in endless ways. Together we collaborated on the four versions of cover art for this series.

Thank you, Jeff Adams, Will Knauss, Kim Smith and Mark Wills. Your online communities, websites, and podcasts are supporting an entire army of independent writers, and for that we all thank you.

Thank you to my parents, Linda, George, and Mary. You always encouraged me to be true to myself, and for that I am eternally grateful.

Thank you to my large network of friends around the globe who continually push me to keep telling stories and sharing life experiences.

Thank you to the readers. Your online reviews and shares have kept this world alive and pushed others to discover it. Please keep sharing!

And finally, thank you, Jan. You reignited the fire in my life. Jag älskar dig!

ABOUT THE AUTHOR

Photo Jan Klingler

A graduate of the University of Tennessee, Jordan Nasser was raised in the South before moving to New York City and then Stockholm, Sweden. His debut novel *Home Is a Fire*, as well as the follow-up novels *The Fire Went Wild* and *This Fire Inside*, all drew from many of his own life experiences. The series has been featured in the *Advocate*, *Paper Magazine*, and the *New York Times,* among others. *Through the Fire* is the fourth and final book in the series.

Mr. Nasser has plans for new projects.

jordannasser.com